Loyalty and Desire

A Mafia Arranged Marriage

BY

Nicolette Chase

Loyalty and Desire

Table of Contents

Chapter 1: Shadows of the Past

I could see the city sprawling beneath me, a ruthless spirit alive with lights and shadows. But even at this height, there was no escaping the gravity of the past year, a tide of events that had reshaped my life, the lives of those I loved… and those who wanted to claim me.

A year had passed since the fateful night when my future had been sewn together in the silence of the family gathering. The moment I'd learned that I was pledged to a man in an arranged marriage.

The man? Dante Moretti.

The mafia world had spent the past year gossiping about it: Dante, a handsome dominant alpha male, heir to a mafia dynasty had agreed to marry me, Alessia Romano, femme fatale, mafia princess. It felt surreal at the time. A calculated decision made by our fathers to strengthen the Moretti family's position in the unforgiving landscape of their criminal empire. It had felt like a decision hammered out in a smoke-filled back room, void of the warmth that should accompany such a union.

I had resigned myself to the path laid before me, secretly grappling with the reality of a life held captive by familial duty.

As I stood gazing out the window, I felt the relentless pull of the past and the promise of the future intertwining. Through all the twists and turns—alliances forged in blood, enemies lurking in the peripheries, and unexpected alliances—I had come to realize that becoming Mrs. Dante Moretti would not simply be an extension of my identity. It would be a transformation, a melding of two powerful forces tangled in a web of loyalty, ambition, and love.

In our private moments, I had discovered a different side of Dante. Beneath the hardened exterior lay a compassionate loyalty that spoke to the depths of my heart. Our relationship had blossomed, a wildflower emerging from cracks in the concrete. He was more than a destined groom; he was becoming a partner, my confidant, my hope for a future unclouded by old-mafia violence and treachery.

"Alessia," a soft voice called from the doorway.

It was Maria, the Moretti family's matriarch and my mother-in-law-to-be. She had mastered the art of her role as wife of the late, great Moretti don. I aspired to be like her and was lucky she had gently taken me under her wing, showing me how to fit in without losing myself in the process.

Her presence brought warmth into the room, her essence like the aromatic smell of fresh bread wafting in from the kitchen. She smiled at me in her kind way. "It's time to prepare for the gathering."

I nodded, drawing a steadying breath. Tonight was pivotal, an exclusive, invite-only charity gala that fronted what tonight was really all about: a show of influence and power. This was the chance for the Moretti empire to flex its influential connections while showing off their mafia heir and his fiancée to all in attendance.

It was a display of unity, a farce, since some of our rival mafia families would be in attendance. Old wealth with just the right amount of dignity and social status would be there just as new money with new power hungry for more would be.

Mafia matriarchs and dons lived for evenings like this. Families from all corners would gather—old allies and potential risers, shadowy figures disguised in tailored suits and sparkling jewels. It was a delicate dance fraught with power shifts and veiled threats, and I needed to make an impression.

I had been raised for moments such as this. I was still learning to embrace them, to master each nuance of small talk.

"Do you need help picking out your dress?" Maria asked gently, her smile reassuring.

"Thank you, but I believe I know what to wear," I replied, forcing a smile while gripping the edge of the window's curtain. I was consumed by a dichotomy of emotions: pride in what I had become and trepidation about the future.

"Tonight is important for our family. You will shine, Alessia," she encouraged, her delicate hands clasped in front of her. "It's essential we present strength and influence to our guests."

"Is that why Giovanni is invited?" I asked, glancing toward her, a sliver of concern edging my voice. Giovanni was not a man to be trusted, and inviting him felt like acknowledging a threat. "To show him we are unafraid?"

"Giovanni believes he holds the cards now to shrink our empire while growing his own, but we will show him we have the upper hand," Maria said confidently, brushing away my worries. "He must see we are undeterred by his past attempts to disrupt our family."

Our family—this sacred union of the Romanos and Morettis.

I nodded, the weight of the past year hanging over me like a dark cloud warning us about impending rain. Giovanni's ambition had threatened our peace with his quiet but erratic maneuvers, but it had also inadvertently reinforced the armor around the Moretti name.

As Maria turned to leave, I headed into my closet, ready to decide what I would wear. I knew this gathering was a theatrical performance, and I had to play my part perfectly. In our world, appearances were everything, especially mine as the fiancée to the great Dante Moretti; they could intimidate an adversary or inspire unwavering loyalty.

Choosing a deep red dress that hugged my figure just enough to command attention while reflecting the strength I had cultivated over the past year, I remembered the countless lessons that had shaped me. My father raised me to be strong and pliable. And so, I was.

In the mirror, I could see evidence of my own evolution since my betrothal to Dante. I was no longer just Alessia, mafia princess, the bride-to-be; I was a woman forged in the fires of this life, ready to face whatever chaos lay ahead.

I stood before the tall mirror, putting the finishing touches on my look for tonight. As I fastened my jewelry and adjusted my hair, I couldn't help but feel the memories flood back—my first encounter with Dante, the lingering awkwardness between us, now transformed into a profound connection. Each memory wove into the fabric of my being, guiding my resolve. He had become a partner in ways I hadn't anticipated.

"Alessia," Dante's voice called softly from the hallway, breaking my contemplation. "Are you ready?"

"With you by my side? Always." I stepped into the hall, meeting his gaze, the warmth in his eyes igniting a spark of confidence within me.

He reached out to take my hand, brushing his lips softly against it. "So beautiful, my bride-to-be. How did I get this lucky?" He shot me a roguish wink and I laughed.

"You can thank our fathers for your good fortune." I wrinkled my nose playfully at him.

"Oh, I do… every… single… day," he said, punctuating the words with kisses from my neck to my cheek to my lips.

The moment was electric, and it solidified my resolve to plaster a smile on my face no matter how many stale conversations awaited me. I placed my hand on his muscled arm. "Let's show them what we are made of."

We descended the grand staircase, the excitement and trepidation melding together, echoing off the marble floors like a heartbeat. Every step was accompanied by whispered conversations between family members, their penchant for gossip palpable. I could feel the gravity of the coming event as though it were a living entity, vibrating with every passing moment.

Upon reaching the estate's ballroom, the vibrant lights reflected off the golden accents and crystal chandeliers as laughter and chatter filled the air. Guests dressed in finely tailored suits and exquisite gowns mingled, a showcase of what our world defined as elegance and power. It was a masquerade of alliances, a hedge against the darkness that loomed if one slipped up.

"Stay close," Dante murmured, his hand gently guiding me through the throng, a protector in every sense of the word.

We moved through the crowd, greetings exchanged with practiced ease. I caught sight of Gino, our fierce ally, engaging in animated conversation with a couple from the Mancini family. Then, there was Marco, talking with Luca, one of our youngest members. Marco's eyes never strayed far from Elena Mancini… a habit he had picked up the past year.

The pleasant laughter and polite exchanges revealed the bonds we had built over the years—legacy and loyalty binding us together.

Then I caught sight of him—the shadow as familiar as it was unwelcome. Giovanni Rivetti stood near the perimeter, a calculating smile on his face as he surveyed the gathering. Silver streaked his hair. Rumor was strong that he was the black sheep of his family, and only now had positioned himself to gain something of power in his family's empire. His presence was ominous, an undercurrent of tension washing over me.

"Keep your composure," Dante whispered, his eyes narrowing as he noted Giovanni's gaze flickering over to us. "He's looking to make a statement."

In that moment, I understood the stakes of the evening— an elaborate chess game where every move could alter the power dynamics of our families. Giovanni's quietly ambitious nature was a dangerous match for the Moretti's resolve.

"Maybe we should…" I began, thinking we could split up and work the room separately. But Dante shook his head, his expression firm and confident.

"No, we stand united. We will not show him any sign of weakness."

With those words echoing in my mind, I squared my shoulders and faced the crowd with renewed strength. Tonight was not just about appeasing Giovanni; it was a celebration— an assertion of our family's identity against a backdrop of ambition, intrigue, and loyalty.

As the charity gala continued in the vast Moretti estate, the rooms filled with energy, laughter, and bubbles of champagne, I felt my heart quicken with anticipation. The hour of shadows and secrets was upon us, and we would weather the storm just as our families had taught us to.

The night mattered less to me for what it promised in terms of family name and power, and more for what it represented in our fight against the darkness. My father taught me that not all mafia families were created equal. I was determined to stand tall as a Romano and soon to be Moretti. With Dante by my side, the shadows of our families' pasts would only serve as reminders of our strength, guiding us toward the future we were ready to fight for, no matter the cost.

Chapter 2: A New Threat - Dante's POV

The sunrise spilled golden light into the Moretti estate, but the warmth barely penetrated the tension swirling within its walls.

Breakfast in the dining room felt disjointed this morning, a stark contrast to the grandiose decor and opulent furnishings that surrounded us. As I sat at the table, absentmindedly pushing a slice of toast around my plate, the gravity of last night's events loomed over me, casting long shadows across my thoughts.

Giovanni's presence at our gathering had rattled the false security we felt that he was mostly bark and very little bite, a man still biding his time until he made a big move. I still felt the weight of his calculated taunts—every one of his mocking words stung like a serrated knife.

He had wormed his way in quietly, disrupting the celebration of our family's strength by his presence. With few words, he showcased his ambitions to reclaim territory he believed belonged to him. I knew Giovanni well enough to be aware that he would not let the opportunity to flex pass.

His family was known for playing the long game, subtly, until they struck in a way that left anyone standing in their path reeling.

"Dante?" The familiar voice pulled me from my thoughts, and I looked up to see my beautiful Alessia entering the dining room, the morning light dancing over her features. Her expression held both determination and an undercurrent of concern. "Are you ready for the meeting?"

"Almost," I replied, forcing a smile despite the knot of anxiety twisting in my stomach. "We need to present a united front today."

She approached, taking a seat across from me, and the warmth of her presence provided a fleeting comfort. Over the past year, our arranged engagement had blossomed into something unexpected—a partnership fueled by shared experiences, vulnerability, and a deepening bond that would see us through the darkest moments.

"I thought you could use this," she said, sliding a steaming cup of coffee across the table to me. "You've barely touched your breakfast."

"Thanks." I took a sip, feeling the warmth burn pleasantly in my throat. "I just have a lot on my mind."

"I know." Alessia's eyes held a wisdom beyond her years, and I could see the resolve shining through her. "But we can't lose focus, especially not now. Giovanni already senses an opening. I think his blustering is a weak attempt at a cover for the Rivetti's real plans."

"Exactly," I replied, my jaw tightening as anger flashed through me. "He won't hit us directly, not yet. He'll make a lot of noise. He'll bide his time, waiting for us to slip up. We need to keep our allies close and demonstrate that we're united."

With Alessia by my side, I felt invigorated, bolstered by her commitment. She had seen the darkness this world harbored and had navigated it with grace and strength. It was these very qualities that drew me closer to her—qualities that made her not just a great match as my future spouse but a formidable ally.

The weight of today's meeting settled heavily on my shoulders. The families would gather soon, and it was crucial we showcased our resolve. If Giovanni attempted to pick off our allies one by one, we would need to prove that loyalty to the Moretti family was steadfast and unwavering.

"Dante!" Marco's voice cut through our conversation as he entered the room, his expression serious. "We need to discuss the latest intel on Giovanni. He's rumored to be making moves into our territory that we need to counter now."

"Gather the others," I instructed, my focus sharpening. "Let's discuss how we serve notice. Giovanni's ambitions end here."

I stood, following Marco into the adjoining room where Gino and a few of our trusted men awaited. Our small circle represented the strength of the Moretti family, forged in blood and loyalty. The moment I entered, their gazes locked onto me, anticipation radiating from them.

"Giovanni has been seen moving in and out of the Rivetti territory," Marco began, his tone grave. "He's not operating alone; he's trying to entice new allies to his cause. Reports suggest he's making deals behind closed doors, attempting to garner support from those who once stood with us."

I clenched my fists, feeling the anger flare within me. "We can't allow him to take back control. We need to remind them why they shouldn't side with him."

Gino nodded. "Word is spreading that he's trying to paint us as weak. Distracted. We need to counter that narrative—not only with words but with actions."

"We'll organize a meeting with our allies," I declared, determination radiating from my voice. "We'll demonstrate that any hint of doubt among our ranks is unfounded. This gathering will take place here, in our home. Giovanni wouldn't dare disrupt a Moretti family meeting."

"Good idea," Marco replied, visibly approving of the plan. "We can't let him think he's outsmarting us. It's time to show him how far we'll go to protect our borders."

The men around me were nodding in unison, a surge of adrenaline filling the room. The time was imminent for us to press Giovanni back into his own zone, but the disorganized approach Giovanni hid behind made his next move hard to predict.

"Find out everything—every ally who is turncoat, every informant he is buying off," I said.

He was cunning—using manipulation and big money to undermine us from within, and we had to be prepared to reevaluate who we could trust.

I felt a flicker of uncertainty at how big this could become but pushed it aside as Alessia entered the room, her presence steadying. "I just spoke with Maria," she said, "and she's implementing additional security measures around the estate. We must be cautious."

"Good," I confirmed, appreciating her foresight. "I hope he wouldn't be so rash as to attempt to come here but better safe than sorry."

Within the inner circle of our family, it was imperative to ensure that no vulnerability went unnoticed. Trust was the bedrock of our operations, but Giovanni had a talent for exploiting weaknesses. The thought sent a chill down my spine.

As we finalized the details of the gathering, I felt the cloth of fate weaving tighter around us. We were standing at a precipice—the possibility of an explosive shift in the balance of power lingered over us. We needed to be ten steps ahead of him, to anticipate his movements before he struck.

"Stay aware of movement outside," I reminded the men, glancing around the room, feeling the weight of their gaze. "We can't let our guards down. Each one of us is critical to the safety of our family."

With the plan set into motion, the air shifted from anxious anticipation to resolute determination. We were not merely defending our territory; we were safeguarding our legacy, our honor, our way of life.

I turned to Alessia as the men filed out, her expression steady yet contemplative. "Are you okay?" I asked, sensing the tension still swirling within her.

"Just thinking," she replied, her tone reflective. "What if Giovanni tries to rattle our allies? He's a slippery one. We can't give in to fear."

"We'll be vigilant," I affirmed, feeling my resolve deepen.

"We can't afford to lose what we've built. You are part of this family now, Alessia. We protect our own."

"Then let's show them," she replied, determination lighting her features. "We will prove that the Moretti name stands strong against anyone who dares to threaten us."

Together, we stepped out of the office, the energy in the penthouse humming with purpose. I glanced out through one of the large windows, the cityscape stretching before me, vibrant yet treacherous. I could feel Giovanni's presence creeping into the periphery of our lives like a dark cloud, foreboding and persistent. His sudden interest in trying to work his way into our territory is not random. He must be trying to prove himself, to gain a higher ranking in the Rivetti crime family.

As we moved through the halls, my mind raced. Every decision I made would ripple through our world, impacting our future, the lives of our loved ones, and our place within this unforgiving domain.

When we reached the expansive living room, I caught sight of movement outside the penthouse. Turning my gaze toward the street, I noticed a sedan with blacked-out windows lingering near the curb. My instincts kicked into high gear; something about it set off alarm bells in my mind.

"Alessia," I murmured, drawing her attention. "Do you see that car?"

Her expression turned serious as she took a glance outside. "It doesn't belong here, does it? We need to be cautious."

"Stay within the walls of the estate when you're there. Here, my men are watching every entrance," I instructed, my voice low but firm. I felt the weight of my responsibilities bearing down on me. Giovanni was not just a rival; he was a master puppeteer, and I could not let him pull the strings that governed our fate.

"I won't hide," Alessia replied defiantly, determination resolute. "I'm a part of this family. I will stand with you."

"Then let's not show weakness," I said, a surge of pride swelling within me. Together, we would face whatever challenges lay ahead, fortified by the bond we shared and the loyalty ingrained in our hearts.

As we collectively prepared for our meeting with allies, building walls against the encroaching shadows of uncertainty, I realized this was no longer just about power—it was about protecting our family, our legacy, and the strength that came from enduring together.

The time for skirmishes was over; it was now about fortifying our position against a threat that loomed larger than any single man. Giovanni's threats to our territory had awakened the beast within us, and we would not back down. The Moretti family would rise, fighting side by side, unbreakable in our resilience. Shadows would not conquer us; we would defy them, creating our own destiny amidst the chaos.

Together, we would face the storm.

Chapter 3: Trust Issues - Dante's POV

The Moretti empire had built its foundations on intricately woven threads of loyalty and ambition. From the marble hallways of the penthouse to the bustling streets of New York, every corner of our territory echoed with the legacy of my family: a consortium of reputable businesses ranging from restaurant chains to high-stakes investments in construction and logistics. But interwoven through the tapestry of success lay the inherent complexities of trust and betrayal, particularly in the shadowy world of organized crime.

As I stood in the heart of our main office, the weight of responsibility crashed over me like an ocean wave. The walls were adorned with photographs of past triumphs—openings of new restaurants, successful partnerships, and family milestones. Each image captured a moment of pride, but beneath the veneer of accomplishment lay a murky world fraught with danger. The dining tables where we served lasagna were often the same tables where plans for less savory operations were sketched out—extortion, protection rackets, and the like.

"Dante!" A voice broke through my thoughts, and I turned to see Gino striding into the room, his expression tense. He was one of my most trusted men, fiercely loyal but often weighed down by the burdens of the business. "We need to talk about Rivetti's people. They're making moves deeper into our territory."

"What have you heard?" I asked, a deep sense of concern resonating within me. Giovanni had been testing boundaries since our last confrontation, and I hated the idea of letting him take a foothold in our operations.

"They're trying to cut in on our logistics contracts. Just last week, one of our drivers was threatened while making deliveries on the West Side," Gino explained, his eyes narrowing. "They're trying to set up shop without drawing attention."

I clenched my jaw, the fury bubbling beneath the surface. Our logistics business was a cornerstone of our operations. It provided the veins through which our empire flowed—

ensuring that the restaurants were stocked, that we maintained the upper hand in the supply chain, and it generated substantial revenue. Allowing Giovanni to encroach on that territory was not just a threat; it was an affront.

"How many of his men are involved?" I asked, my voice laced with urgency.

"Sources say at least five, possibly more. They're trying to undermine us, but I'm not sure who else might be helping him," Gino stated. "We need to address this before it festers."

The issue of loyalty was intricate. The capacity for betrayal existed in every alliance, whether forged in the cigar lounge or the boardroom.

"I want full surveillance on all our operations—monitor the deliveries, keep tabs on our drivers, and report any unusual encounters," I ordered, feeling the severity of the moment. "We can't afford to lose what we've worked so hard to establish. I want every report on my desk by the end of the week."

"Understood," Gino replied, a flicker of gratitude in his eyes. He shared my concerns, understanding that our empire thrived not just on strength but trust, and Giovanni was keenly aware of that.

As Gino left the office, I turned my attention to the large windows overlooking the city. The world outside bustled with activity, but inside my mind, I was calculating risks. The arrangements we had made with other families and the businesses we supported through charitable contributions had enabled us to stand beside those we counted as allies. Each relationship we built had to be monitored for signs of weakness and potential treachery.

The families involved in our businesses were not mere associates; they were interwoven into the fabric of our lives. They relied on us, and we on them. And yet, connections also came with their own set of fears. A misstep, a moment of arrogance could unravel everything we had built over generations.

I snapped back to reality when Marco entered, a look of determination etched across his face. "Dante, I've completed the rounds of our restaurants and spoke with the managers. They're starting to sense the pressure from Rivetti's crew. This tension could unsettle our operations."

"Did anyone express reservations about their safety?" I asked, my heart pounding. If Giovanni's tactics spread fear among our workforce, it could damage morale and hinder productivity.

"Some of the staff are uneasy. They've heard whispers. We need to reassure them, provide a united front," Marco said, clearly troubled by the implications of Giovanni's interference. "We should consider a family meeting."

I nodded, appreciating Marco's insight. The family businesses were more than just financial ventures; they were symbols of our legacy. The restaurants—a chain of beloved establishments serving authentic Italian cuisine—had become the lifeblood of our name, beloved in the community for both their quality and the familial atmosphere crafted meticulously over time.

But the moment trust began to falter, so did the foundation upon which our empire stood. It was essential to confront these issues head-on, especially with the dangers swirling around us.

"I'll gather everyone this evening," I decided. "We'll address the concerns and reassure our staff of our commitment. We cannot let Giovanni's actions create fractures among us."

"Agreed," Marco responded, his features tightening. "We must also make sure that everyone is clear on our policy— loyalty will be honored, but those who show weakness will not be tolerated. We can't afford to coddle anyone."

Every word Marco spoke resonated deeply within me. Trust was a double-edged sword; while it primed unfaltering loyalty, it could also be exploited. Giovanni knew this game, and if he could instill distrust in our ranks, that would be his path to victory.

After discussing the logistics, I made my way to the family meeting room. Large, heavy oak tables occupied the center of the room, surrounded by plush leather chairs that had borne the weight of many decisions. I let out a slow breath and steadied myself; tonight's discussion would guide our future.

As the clock ticked closer to the hour, the family began to filter in—Gino, Marco, and a handful of others I respected deeply; men who had proven their loyalty time and again. The walls stemming from the floor felt strong, an invulnerable fortress. But I knew better; nothing was truly invincible.

"Thank you all for coming," I began, my voice steady as they settled into their seats. "I know we've faced challenges recently—challenges that threaten not only our operations but the integrity of our family. Rivetti is stepping up his game, trying to exploit any sign of weakness."

I paused, studying their expressions. I saw the flickers of resolve, of determination—the men around me were loyal to a fault. "But we will not allow this to become a cancer that spreads in our ranks. We have built this empire on trust and loyalty, and we need to stand firm."

I proceeded to outline the recent developments concerning Rivetti's encroachments, detailing the threats against our businesses. Their concern was palpable, the weight of what was at stake settling over us like an oppressive fog.

"Tonight, I need your commitment to maintain security and support our staff," I continued, a fire igniting within me. "We must ensure that everyone knows they are part of the family. If any scandals arise, they will not remain in isolation; we will address them together, united."

"This is our home," Gino added, his voice laden with passion. "We must protect it. Giovanni's actions are not just business; they're a direct attack on our legacy."

"Agreed," Marco chimed in, fervor igniting in his words. "We need to let the community know we stand together. It's time to rally them and show Rivetti that he can't step into our domain unchecked. It's more than business for us; it's personal."

The unity in the room surged, igniting a collective resolve. We were not merely defending businesses; we were protecting a legacy forged through blood, sweat, and tears. Giovanni's threat drew us closer, solidifying our bonds, reminding us of the importance of family.

As the meeting progressed, I felt the fire pulsing within, each affirmation resonating deeper than the last. Every plan made, every strategy discussed, reaffirmed what we ultimately stood for—the honor of the Moretti name. We would face whatever darkness Giovanni sought to cast upon us, banded together as a family, unwavering in our loyalty.

As I looked around the room, I caught glimpses of the strong faces of men I had come to trust, brothers shaped by trials and shared victories. In the heart of our family wasn't just loyalty; it was conviction. Giovanni might lurk in the shadows, but within these walls, we were fortified—a force to be reckoned with, unyielding against the tides of betrayal.

Tonight was just the beginning; we would emerge from this storm not just as survivors but as warriors ready to redefine the game and keep our legacy alive. And in doing so, we would show the world that the Morettis would not back down. Trust would weave us together, each of us a thread stitched tightly in the fabric of our empire, resilient and true.

Chapter 4: Forbidden Love - Marco's POV

The moon hung high in the night sky, a silver coin illuminated against a velvet black canvas, casting soft light over the serpentine streets of New York City. In the air was an electric anticipation, the kind that only seemed to blossom in the moments before something monumental was set to occur.

As darkness enveloped the city, I stood at the window of my apartment, staring out at the shimmering skyline, feeling the weight of the world outside pressing against me.

But the tension gripping my chest wasn't just about the business. It had a different kind of heat—a passion that threatened to consume me whole, intertwined with a yearning that had grown over the years.

Elena.

The name echoed in my mind like a haunting melody, forever intertwined with the chaotic rhythm of my life.

We had danced around each other for so long—friends first, then partners in crime, and somewhere along the way, she had unknowingly become the axis on which my world spun. Elena was not just a daughter of the Mancini family, she was a force of nature—wild, vibrant, and unstoppable. There was a fire in her, a fierce spirit that matched my own, yet it was our families' long-standing history, darkened by alliances and rivalries, that made our connection feel forbidden.

"Marco!" Her voice broke through my thoughts like a sweet bell chiming, and I turned to see her slipping into the apartment, a breath of fresh air against the backdrop of my brooding. She wore a fitted black dress that accentuated her curves and flowed just past her knees, like liquid night draped around her body. It clung to her like a second skin, each movement exuding confidence, grace, and an undeniable allure.

"Hey," I replied, my voice hoarse with restraint as I tried to mask the rush of emotions swirling within me. "You look... stunning."

"Thank you," she said, her cheeks flushing slightly as she stepped closer, those captivating emerald eyes glittering with mischief. "I thought tonight might be interesting after everything that's happened."

I felt my heartbeat quicken, the air around us thickening with unsaid words, a tension that crackled like electricity. We stood inches apart, the space between us charged with the unspoken desires we had both held at bay. "Interesting" was an understatement. Tonight felt like it was set to change everything.

"So, what's the plan?" I asked, trying to retreat into the sanctuary of tactical conversation, though my instincts screamed otherwise.

She tilted her head slightly, a playful smile dancing across her lips. "I came here to talk about Giovanni. But I admit, I've been thinking about more than just business."

Those words sent a jolt through me, igniting every nerve in my body. I was aware of the weight of her gaze, how it seemed to pull me closer, blurring the lines of reason. "What do you mean?" I asked, though the answer lay in the depths of her eyes, shimmering with that familiar reckless exuberance.

"I want to talk about us," she said softly, stepping closer, closing the distance that had increasingly become unbearable. "I can't pretend I don't feel this anymore, Marco."

Her honesty acted like a key, unlocking the floodgate that had held my feelings in check for too long. "Neither can I," I admitted, stepping forward until we were mere breaths apart. "But we both know the implications."

"The implications don't matter to me," she confessed, her voice falling to a whisper as she gazed up at me. "Not when I feel this way about you."

The world outside fell away, and all that remained was the pulse of urgency between us. I had tried to resist—for the sake of our families, for the sake of tradition—but stepping into the orbit of her emotions was a siren's call I could no longer ignore.

I leaned down, closing the distance, my lips capturing hers with fierce hunger. The kiss was raw, igniting an inferno that surged through my veins. She melted against me, her warmth enveloping me, stealing my breath and weaving our souls into an unbreakable bond.

As I deepened the kiss, Elena responded with equal fervor, her fingers threading through my hair, drawing me closer. The soft sigh that escaped her lips sent a rush of fire coursing through me—a potent reminder of everything we had kept buried beneath layers of expectation and duty.

We broke apart, our foreheads resting against each other as we caught our breath, the reality of our situation crashing in. "Marco, we can't hide this forever," she murmured, a vulnerability threading through her courage.

"What if they find out?" I asked, concern flickering within me. Our families were entwined in a million ways, bonds steeped in history, and the thought of our love being weaponized against us sent a chill racing down my spine.

"Then we fight," she said, her voice resolute. "I refuse to let our families dictate what my heart wants. I care about you, Marco. That's all that should matter."

Her defiance stirred something deep within me—a longing to embrace this truth we had tiptoed around for too long. It was maddening and exhilarating, and I could feel the flame of passion rekindling as I captured her lips once more, kissing her with a fervor that spoke the truths of my heart.

"I don't want to lose you," I muttered against her mouth, the confession slipping out more desperately than I intended.

"You won't," she replied fiercely, her breath warm against my lips. With that, she pulled me back into the depths of passion, fueling the desires that surged like liquid fire between us. It felt like we were stepping into a world of our own, insulated against the demands of the chaos outside.

With a gentle persistence, I led her to the living area, where the city lights flickered like stars—striking against the backdrop of the night. As we fell onto the soft couch, the weight of the world seemed to dissolve around us, leaving nothing but us and the heat spiraling between us.

"Marco," she sighed, her fingers tracing patterns across my chest, igniting every nerve ending in the process. "This feels right… being with you like this."

I captured her chin, tilting her head up gently, our eyes locking as I whispered, "I've wanted this for so long." Then, with a surge of boldness, I leaned closer, kissing her again, deeper this time, intertwining our souls.

The kiss burned with an urgency that felt intoxicating. My hands found their way to her waist, pulling her closer, as if we could fuse our beings into one. There was a wildness, a recklessness in the air. I couldn't, I wouldn't, hold back.

With deliberate savagery, I pushed her back against the couch cushions, my body covering hers as desire surged like wildfire. Our kisses deepened, exploring and tasting one another, each breath a testament to the passion that had built between us over all these months.

Elena responded fervently, her hands clawing at my shirt, tugging me closer as she let out soft gasps of pleasure. My heart raced as I traced my lips down from her mouth to her neck, planting fiery kisses along her collarbone, relishing in the softness of her skin.

"Marco," she breathed, the sound resonating deep within me, driving me forward. "Please."

With every plea, she stoked the flames of our desire. I lifted her dress slightly, letting my hands roam over her bare, soft thighs, feeling her shiver beneath my touch. There was a thrill of danger in this moment—time seemed suspended as we disregarded everything else and surrendered to the passion that demanded release.

"Are you sure about this?" I murmured against her skin, stealing glances up at her face. Her eyes sparkled with determination, urging me onward.

"More than anything," she insisted, arching her body closer, encouraging me to explore her further. It didn't take long for the world around us to fade completely, leaving behind only the heavy intimacy we shared.

The primal need pulling us together surged like a beast awakening from slumber. I captured her lips again, deepening the kiss, and she surrendered entirely, her body melting against mine. It was an intoxicating fusion of passion as we unraveled together, skin on skin, hearts racing dangerously close to the edge.

Time blurred as we moved in rhythm, the outside world vanishing beyond the walls of the apartment. Each kiss, each caress felt like a breath of fresh air—a reminder that something beautiful could bloom amidst the chaos. As she clung to me, her fingers gripping my shoulders, I understood that this love was a reckless, beautiful rebellion against the confines of duty and tradition.

Our connection ignited like a match to kindling—burning fiercely, unrelenting. In that moment, nothing else mattered. It was just Elena and me, intertwined in fire, passion, and a love that defied everything else. As the city roared below us, we forged our own destiny, daring the shadows of our families to challenge our bond.

The night wore on, and despite the looming uncertainties, I knew we would face them together. I held her close, wrapping her in my arms as we drifted into a blissful surrender. Let the world outside fade while we lost ourselves in a love that felt forbidden yet irrepressibly real. The stakes were high, but in each other, we had found sanctuary amidst the storm.

Chapter 5: Unexpected Pregnancy - Alessia's POV

The sun glimmered through the tall windows of the penthouse, casting warm rays across the marble floors and illuminating the modern furnishings of the living room. I stood there, transfixed by the cityscape outside—a vibrant maze of skyscrapers and bustling streets—yet I felt far removed from the world beyond the glass. The air in the room felt heavy, as if charged with an unspoken tension that mirrored the swirling emotions within me.

It had been a rollercoaster of a few weeks since our confrontation with Giovanni at the charity event. The weight of his looming threat still cast shadows over our lives, but now there was another weight I carried—one that filled me with both joy and fear. I wrapped my arms around myself, feeling the soft fabric of my dress against my skin, but it did little to quell the fluttering in my stomach. I was terrified, overwhelmed by the enormity of a revelation that had come crashing into my life: I was pregnant.

Taking a deep breath, I turned away from the window, forcing myself to concentrate. I had known for a few days now, and each passing moment seemed to amplify the excitement mixed with anxiety. I had watched the small change in myself with a blend of wonder and disbelief. This tiny life growing inside me was a miracle, but it also represented everything I had feared: the potential upheaval of my carefully curated world.

As I prepared breakfast in the spacious kitchen, the aroma of freshly brewed coffee filled the air, but it did little to soothe my racing heart. Each sound amplified my nerves—the bubbling of the pot, the sizzle of eggs in the pan—as they echoed the thoughts spinning around in my mind. How would Dante react? Would he be happy? Would he feel overwhelmed? The stakes were high, and I knew this revelation would not just alter our lives, but it could also influence the fragile dynamics of our families and the ever-looming threat from Giovanni.

"Alessia?" Dante's voice broke through my thoughts, rich with concern and curiosity. I turned to see him leaning against the doorway, his expression shifting from relaxed to alert as he noticed my unease. "Is everything okay?"

"Yeah, just… thinking," I replied, forcing a smile, though my heart pounded like a drum. The sight of him sent a rush of warmth through me, but the weight of what I had to reveal nearly paralyzed me.

He walked over, brushing his fingers along the counter as he approached. "You're worried. I can see it. What's on your mind?"

I took a deep breath, gathering my courage. "I need to talk to you about something important." My voice wavered slightly, and I cursed my nerves.

"Sounds serious." He leaned closer, his concern deepening. "What is it, Alessia?"

I could feel the moment stretching out like an eternity, the reality of my news crashing over me again. "I'm pregnant," I finally blurted out, the words spilling from my lips as if pulled by an invisible force.

His eyes widened, surprise etching across his handsome features as the weight of my confession sank in. "Pregnant?" he repeated, the word hanging in the air like a suspended note.

"Yes," I affirmed, my heart racing at the sudden rush of emotions swirling in his gaze. "I took the test this morning. It was positive."

A silence enveloped us, thick with unspoken thoughts before his initial shock morphed into something deeper. I held my breath, watching as various emotions crossed his face—disbelief, fear, and then a flicker of happiness that glimmered like a beacon.

"Wow," Dante breathed, stepping back slightly as he processed the information. "Are you… are you sure?"

"I am sure," I replied, my voice steadier now, though my heart still raced. "I've never been more certain about anything in my life."

He stepped closer once more, taking my hands in his and squeezing gently, as if grounding himself in reality. "Alessia, this is…" His voice trailed off, and I could see him struggling to find the right words.

"I know it's unexpected," I said, feeling the weight of uncertainty creeping back in. "And I know we have a lot to contend with—our families' expectations, Giovanni's threats, everything."

Dante's gaze didn't waver from mine, and in those hazel depths, I saw a mix of fear and determination. "But we've faced so much together," he said, the passion in his voice surfacing. "We can face this too. You and I… we'll figure it out. We have to."

The swell of love I felt for him surged, pushing away some of my fears. "You're right. I just want what's best for our child. To ensure they grow up in a world filled with love and not surrounded by chaos and rivalry."

Dante nodded, the gentle resolve on his face both comforting and invigorating. "We will protect our child from everything. I won't allow them to be part of this life's darker side."

His words brought a rush of confidence to the forefront of my mind. This life—it was our choice to shape it, our duty to create a future that was safe and nurturing for our family. "I want them to have your strength, Dante," I admitted softly, my voice gripping with emotion. "A future grounded in love and resilience."

A smile broke through the concern etched on his face, illuminating his features. "With you as their mother, they'll inherit a legacy that's much more than just our families' histories. They'll inherit love, loyalty, and strength—that's who we are, together."

Together.

The city stretched beyond the windows, its golden lights flickering like distant stars. But none of it mattered. Not the skyline. Not the war raging outside these walls.

Only him.

Dante stood before me, his eyes locked onto mine, his expression soft. But I felt his pulse beneath my fingers, steady and strong, as I pressed his hand against my stomach. He smiled.

"I can't believe I'm pregnant, Dante…" My voice barely came out, thick with emotion.

His fingers curled over mine, his touch warm, grounding. "Say it again."

I swallowed, my heart pounding. "I'm pregnant."

A tremor ran through him, his breath catching. His palm flattened over my stomach, holding me there as if he could already feel the life growing inside me.

A child. Our child.

Dante lifted his gaze, his hands framing my face with a touch that made my chest ache. "I swear to you, I will protect you. Both of you."

Then he kissed me, sealing the promise with something deeper than words. His lips claimed mine, fierce and unyielding, and I let myself fall into him, into us.

His kiss was fire and devotion, a vow only we could understand. I clung to him, my fingers sliding into his hair, desperate to hold onto this moment, to keep him close.

The world outside didn't matter. The wars, the bloodshed, the enemies waiting in the dark. Right now, it was just Dante and me.

He broke the kiss just enough to rest his forehead against mine, his breath warm against my lips. "Alessia, you're mine. And I'm yours. Nothing—no man, no war—will ever take this from us."

I pressed closer, whispering against his mouth, "We are a family now."

His breath shuddered, and he exhaled slowly, his hands slipping back to my stomach. This time, his touch was softer, reverent. "A family," he repeated, the word thick with meaning.

I felt it then—the depth of his love, the weight of his promise. Dante would kill for me. He would die for me.

But he would never lose me.

And I would never let him go.

I shivered as my clothes fell to the floor. This powerful man—my man—was claiming me, right here, right now. With effortless strength he lifted me onto the desk, freeing himself from his pants.

His lips brushed kisses down my neck to my chest, pausing to capture each breast before impatiently, I pulled his body to mine. I gasped as he slid into me. This was heaven. Him and me, together, building a future for us, for our child.

In the aftermath of our lovemaking I nestled my head against his muscled chest. He was happy we were going to have a child, but would the rest of the family think it was too soon?

"I just hope our families can accept this," I admitted, pulling back to look at him.

"I won't let our child be a pawn in some game of power struggles," he said fiercely, the conviction in his tone sending shivers down my spine. "Once we reveal this, we'll stand together. We'll show them that family matters above all else."

Emotions surged forward, and I wrapped my arms around him tightly. "I don't know what I would do without you," I murmured, burying my face in the crook of his neck, breathing in his comforting scent.

"You'll never have to find out," he assured me, his warmth enveloping me in comfort. "We face this together, no matter what. You have my word."

Once we were dressed, a sudden knock on the door broke through our tender moment, startling us both. My heart raced with the realization that it could be anyone—Gino, Marco, or even Giovanni's men. The outside world had the potential to disrupt our precious moment.

"Alessia, it's Maria," came the voice of my future mother-in-law from the other side of the door.

I pulled back slightly, glancing at Dante, who nodded in understanding. "We'll have to address this. But first, can we take a moment just to breathe?"

"Of course," I replied, staying close as I composed myself. I took a deep breath, feeling the weight of my news still lingering, but fortified by our shared resolve.

Dante stepped back, his eyes still shimmering with the joy and anxiety of the moment we shared. "Let's handle this together. We'll find a way to tackle everything one step at a time."

I nodded, intertwining my fingers with his for a moment, grounding myself. The world around us remained tumultuous, laden with challenges, and yet, amidst it all, there was hope blossoming within.

As I opened the door, I prepared to face whatever the day would bring, determined to carve out a future where our love flourished despite the shadows lurking outside. I was ready to embrace this unexpected journey, knowing we would navigate it together.

With Dante by my side, together we would build a life full of love and strength. No matter how daunting the circumstances, our love would remain the cornerstone of our world, a beacon of light illuminating the path ahead. The news of my pregnancy was not just a twist of fate; it was the start of our legacy—a beautiful beginning to a new chapter in our intertwined lives.

Chapter 6: Confessions and Revelations - Dante's POV

The penthouse was quiet, the only sound the distant hum of the city beyond the windows. I leaned against the cool marble of the kitchen counter, a mug of black coffee cradled between my hands. The aroma wafted up, bitter and rich, pulling me back to the reality of the moment.

Just days ago, Alessia had shared the life-changing news of her pregnancy, and now I found myself standing at a precipice, both excited and terrified of the future.

The past few weeks had thrown everything into disarray. Giovanni's threats loomed just as heavily as the new life growing within Alessia, intertwining our fates in ways that felt both exhilarating and daunting. I exhaled sharply as I recalled the look of joy mingled with apprehension in her eyes when she revealed her news. It was a moment I would carry with me forever, a memory etched into my heart, and it was clear to me that we both had much to consider.

"Dante?" Alessia's voice broke through the silence, bright and warm, pulling me from my thoughts. I turned to see her walking into the kitchen, her presence lighting up the room in a way that had always captivated me. Even now, with the changes our lives were undergoing, she held a strength that made it impossible for me to look away.

"Hey," I said, lifting my mug as if it might offer me some semblance of calm. "How are you feeling this morning?"

"I'm okay," she replied, stepping closer. Her hand rested against the counter as she leaned in, her expression shifting from casual to something more serious. "I've been thinking a lot about everything we talked about."

"Yeah, me too," I admitted, setting my coffee down to give her my full attention. I could see the gears turning in her head, the weight of our impending parenthood settling heavily on her shoulders.

"What if Giovanni finds out?" she asked, her voice barely above a whisper, but the fear in her eyes was unmistakable. "What if he uses this against us?"

I stepped closer, instinctively wanting to reassure her. "We have to be careful, but we can't let fear dictate our lives. If he finds out, we'll handle it together. We always have."

She nodded, though the tension remained etched in her features. "I just don't want our child to be a pawn in this twisted game. I want them to have a chance at a good life, away from all the chaos."

"Me too," I said, my resolve hardening. "And I promise, we'll create that life for our child. But we need to strengthen our position first. We can't show any signs of vulnerability."

Alessia studied me for a moment, her gaze piercing. "What do you mean?"

"I think we need to be proactive. We have allies within our families, but we also need to make sure they remain loyal. We can't let Giovanni play us against one another," I explained. "The sooner we solidify our relationships, the stronger our foundation will be."

"What are you suggesting?" she asked, curiosity flickering in her eyes.

"I want to call a family meeting," I said, my heart racing at the thought. "To reaffirm our alliances, to ensure everyone knows what's at stake. A united front is more important than ever now."

"You're right," she agreed, and I felt a swell of pride in her understanding. "Let's do it. We'll gather everyone we trust. But, Dante… can we also talk to them about our child? I don't want to hide it."

"I think we should," I replied, though uncertainty lingered in my mind. "But we have to frame it carefully. Giovanni will no doubt try to use this against us. We need to present it as a testament to our commitment to one another."

The thought of bringing our families together was both exhilarating and terrifying. I could feel the tendrils of unease swirling in my stomach, but the determination in Alessia's eyes pushed me forward.

"Alright," I said finally, my heart racing with urgency. "Let's gather Gino and Marco first. We can brainstorm how we want to approach this announcement."

"Perfect," she said, a spark of enthusiasm igniting within her. I felt grateful that, despite the circumstances, we had each other to rely on.

As we moved through the apartment, the air between my beautiful fiancée and me crackled with energy. I observed every little detail in Alessia's demeanor—the way she carried herself, the confidence seeping back into her, reflecting her undeniably fierce spirit. Just being near her felt like a lifeline, reminding me that together, we could face anything.

A few moments later, Gino and Marco arrived. I gestured for them to take a seat at the dining table, my heart racing in anticipation. As we settled in, I couldn't help but feel the weight of the discussion ahead.

"Thanks for coming on short notice," I said, trying to gauge their reactions.

"Of course, Dante," Gino replied, always the steady one among us. "What's going on?"

Alessia took a deep breath, and I took her hand in mine, squeezing gently for support. "We have some significant news to share," she began, her voice steady and resolute.

"We're expecting a child." The words flowed from her lips with a clarity that left no room for doubt.

The silence that followed was palpable, and I watched as Gino's eyebrows shot up in surprise, while Marco's expression shifted to one of joyous disbelief. "Wow, congratulations!" Marco exclaimed, a smile breaking across his face. "That's incredible news!"

I felt the tension ease slightly at their excitement and the genuine support shining in their eyes. "We wanted to bring you in on this now because it changes everything," I continued, looking at each of them in turn. "We need to unite—not just as a family, but as a coalition against the threats facing us."

"Giovanni won't take this lightly," Gino cautioned, the seriousness creeping back into his gaze. "He'll likely see this as an opportunity to exploit any weaknesses."

"That's why we're here," Alessia added, her voice strong. "This child will not be a bargaining chip. We need to ensure our alliances are strong, and we need to make it clear that our family comes first."

Marco nodded, his expression shifting to one of determination. "We'll support you. If Giovanni tries anything, we'll have your backs."

"Thank you," I said, feeling a profound sense of relief wash over me. This feeling of community, of shared responsibility, ignited a fire deep within me. "But we must prepare carefully. We need to frame our message without showing any signs of vulnerability. We need to assure everyone that this child is a blessing—a new chapter for the Moretti family."

"Agreed," Gino said, leaning forward. "I suggest we call a meeting that includes the Mancinis. A united front will only reinforce how serious we are. This will set the tone for any future interactions regarding Giovanni."

As plans began to take shape, I felt the burden of my earlier fears begin to lift. Each word spoken in that room felt like a protective shield forming around us; every shared idea crafted an unbreakable barrier of defense.

"I also think we should make a point to connect with some of the families that have been loyal to us," Alessia suggested, her gaze unwavering. "We'll want to solidify those ties now to show strength from the get-go."

"Yes," Marco agreed. "We can't leave any stone unturned. If we can establish your child as proof of endurance and growth within the family legacy, it will lend legitimacy to our position."

The conversation continued, driven by a spirited determination that spread from Alessia to Gino, Marco, and back to me. I could feel the tide shifting in our favor, and with each passing moment, the weight of impending fatherhood transformed from something overwhelming into a source of endless possibilities.

As the meeting wrapped up, I couldn't shake the feeling of hope blooming within me, overshadowing every fear and doubt that had clouded my mind. Our child would be a beacon—a sign of resilience amid the chaos surrounding us.

When Gino and Marco finally left, I turned to Alessia, who looked more vibrant than I had seen in days. "You're incredible, you know that?" I murmured, my heart swelling with admiration.

"Me? You're the one who had the brilliant idea to call the meeting!" She laughed softly, her eyes shimmering with joy and acceptance.

"And you're the one who has given me a reason to fight, to grow and to protect." I stepped closer and wrapped my arms around her, pulling her in tightly. I could feel the warmth radiate between us, igniting a connection that was palpable and pure.

"Together, we can face anything," she whispered, resting her head on my shoulder. I held her close and closed my eyes, grounding myself in the moment.

In that embrace, I felt the love and hope surge, illuminating the uncertainty that had once clouded my heart. We were embarking on a new journey, one filled with challenges and promises.

As we prepared to face Giovanni and the others, I couldn't shake the feeling that our family was destined to rise. Together, we would create a legacy steeped in love and strength and fight fiercely for our future.

Chapter 7: Rising Tensions - Elena's POV

The sun hung low in the sky, casting an orange glow over the city as I stood on the balcony of my apartment, gripping the railing with white knuckles. Below me, the streets throbbed with life, a cacophony of honking horns, laughter, and snippets of conversation, but up here, I was enveloped by a suffocating silence. The moment of serenity was a stark contrast to the turmoil churning inside me.

My family's world had always been steeped in complexities, but since the news of Alessia's pregnancy broke, I felt the ground shift beneath me. I had watched Dante and Alessia navigate their new reality with strength and determination, yet it only served to amplify my own feelings of inadequacy and doubt, emotions that now twisted in a relentless spiral within me.

The truth was hard to swallow: Dante was moving forward with his life, expanding his family, while I remained stuck in a web of uncertainties—a tangled mess of aspiration and unfulfilled desires. I wanted to be happy for them, for the love they shared and the future the unborn child represented, but with every passing day, the knot of jealousy tightened within my chest.

Why was I dragging my feet while they soared ahead? It felt as if the walls were closing in, a quiet panic creeping into my heart. I drew in a deep breath, trying to gather my thoughts, but the fear that my own dreams were slipping away was too overwhelming.

"Hey." Marco's voice cut through the haze of my thoughts as he stepped outside, leaning against the doorframe. The familiar warmth in his tone had always offered solace, but today I felt raw, unguarded. "You alright?"

I turned to him, forcing a smile that didn't quite reach my eyes. "I'm fine," I said, though my voice betrayed me, wavering on the edge of truth.

"Doesn't seem like it," he replied, studying me intently. "Talk to me. What's going on?"

Silence enveloped us as I weighed my options. I could hide behind a façade, pretend everything was fine, but I could sense that Marco saw through the cracks. Our bond ran deep, yet the fear of burdening him with my insecurities held me back.

"I just… I don't know," I finally admitted, my voice barely above a whisper. "Everything feels chaotic right now. Alessia and Dante are so focused on the future, and I…" I hesitated, realizing how exposed I felt already. "I feel like I'm standing still."

Marco tilted his head gently, allowing me to gather my thoughts. "You're not standing still. You're here, with me. We're in this together," he said, conviction layered in his tone. "What do you want? Because I'm here to help you get there."

I swallowed hard, battling the swell of emotions rising within me. I had always coveted the closeness Marco and I shared, the deep bond of trust that allowed us to navigate the treacherous waters of our families' expectations. But the currents of jealousy and self-doubt were threatening to pull me under.

"It's just… I've always wanted more," I admitted, letting my vulnerability surface. "More than just being part of our families' plans. I want my own life, my own ambitions. But now, with everything changing so rapidly, I feel like I'm being left behind."

For a moment, Marco studied me in silence, and I could see his wheels turning. "Do you mean… you want a child?" he asked cautiously, the thought lingering in the air between us.

The question hung heavy, and I felt a rush of heat flood my cheeks. "Sometimes I do. I mean, I love children." My voice trailed off as I recalled moments shared with kids in our families—laughter and innocence mingling together. But the weight of the reality hit hard. "But is it the right time? Would I be able to give them everything they deserve?"

"None of us ever really know the right time, Elena. Trust me, we're all figuring it out as we go along," he reassured, stepping closer, his presence enveloping me in comfort. "Alessia is having a baby, and while that's great, it doesn't diminish who you are or what you aspire to be."

"But it feels like it sometimes," I confessed, frustration boiling to the surface. "I don't want to be defined by my association with our family or stop pursuing my own dreams."

He nodded slowly, taking in my words. "You have to fight for what you want, whatever that may be. If you want a family someday, you need to make that a priority. But if you want to invest in your career or explore other paths, you can't let family dynamics dictate your choices. You deserve happiness on your terms."

A flicker of hope came to life within me, brightening the darkness my jealousy had cast. "You're right," I said, my voice steadier, though doubts murmured at the corners of my mind. "I just don't want to push anyone aside to pursue my ambitions. I want to be there for Alessia and Dante."

"We all want that," he reassured, a hint of a smile dancing on his lips. "These are challenging times. But while you're supporting them, don't forget about yourself, too."

"I know," I replied, frustration still clouding my mind. "I just feel so conflicted. What am I supposed to do while everyone else has their lives unfolding? It's hard to watch—like I'm stuck in a limbo of my own making."

Marco paused, taking a moment to consider my words. "Would it help if we brainstorm goals together? I can help you figure out what steps to take next, no matter the direction."

The idea hung in the air, a glimmering light amidst the turmoil I felt. "You'd do that?" My voice caught as I considered the effort and support he was willing to provide.

"Of course," he said earnestly. "You're family. I want you to be happy, to find fulfillment. I'll do whatever it takes to help you get there."

"Thank you, Marco." The sincerity in his eyes chased away some of my unease, fortifying me against the rising tension inside. There was beauty in my relationships with those around me, and I was grateful to have someone as supportive as him.

"Let's meet later," he suggested, a grin creeping onto his lips. "We can create a plan—and maybe even brainstorm some next steps for you. You deserve to pursue your dreams, too."

As I nodded, I felt a renewed sense of hope beginning to blossom within me. Perhaps I wasn't destined to be stuck in the shadows; perhaps I could carve my own path alongside my friends and family. The uncertainty surrounding my life choices felt like an unwieldy monster, but it could be tackled bit by bit.

As the evening drew near, I felt lighter. I had shared my burden, my conflict, my dreams with Marco, and if it turned out we could help one another, perhaps we could find a way through the tangled mess of family and expectations.

Later that evening, I gathered my thoughts, organizing ideas around what I wanted to achieve. Would I pursue my career more aggressively? Would I explore family life sooner than I thought? The possibilities seemed vast as I began to chart my own future, free from the constraints that had once smothered me.

The air hummed with energy, each revelation shedding light on a path ahead that had previously felt obscured. I knew that rising tensions and emotions could threaten to pull me down, but with Marco's unwavering support, I felt strengthened.

Finally, I had a clearer vision, both of my aspirations and what I wanted from life beyond the family legacy—a desire for autonomy and happiness that refused to be muted.

Tonight marked the beginning of my journey in pursuit of my dreams, and no matter what lay ahead—whether that involved starting a family or chasing career goals—I would embrace my future with resolve. Life might include chaos, but within it, I would carve out a world that was uniquely mine, and I was ready to embrace whatever came next.

Chapter 8: Security Dilemma - Alessia's POV

The night pressed in around me as I stood in the expansive living room of the Moretti penthouse, the city lights twinkling like stars below. The skyline had always brought me comfort, a reminder of the life we had forged amidst the chaos. But now, with all that was happening, it felt like a fortress surrounded by turbulence. As I paced the room, I felt the weight of my responsibilities pressing down on my shoulders like an invisible cloak.

Dante and I had been preparing to face our families, and I knew the battle for our future was only just beginning. Giovanni's predatory ambitions were growing bolder, and the threat loomed larger than ever. Caught in the whirlwind of organized crime, it took less than a whisper to trigger a series of destructive events, and I was painfully aware of how delicate our situation was.

"Alessia!" Dante called from the kitchen, pulling me from my thoughts. "Can you come here for a second? I need your input on something."

"Of course!" I replied, hurrying toward him, my heart racing at the possibility of brainstorming solutions to our security dilemma. As I entered the kitchen, I found him sitting at the table, his laptop open, scattered papers framing him like a chaotic mind map of our predicament.

"Look at this." He gestured to the screen, and I leaned closer, frowning at the data displayed—charts tracking the recent drug routes and gambling operations running through our territory. "We need to address the vulnerabilities in our security, especially with what Giovanni has been trying to pull. He's been pushing harder to take control of our businesses, one subtle infiltration at a time, specifically with the drug routes."

My stomach twisted. The drug trade had plagued our family for years, spawning rivalries and chaos, and it was especially volatile right now with tensions brewing between our territories. "I hate that we're even in a position to be vulnerable," I admitted, my voice laced with frustration. "This is our home, our life. How can we let Giovanni encroach on what we've built?"

"Exactly," Dante replied, his jaw tightening. "I've gathered intel on how the Rivetti family has been seeking out alliances with other criminal enterprises, particularly in the drug trade. They're attempting to leverage existing routes to undermine our hold. If they gain a foothold in our territory, it could spell disaster for everything we've worked for."

I wanted to scream in frustration, but instead, I drew in a deep breath, steeling myself against the chaos lurking just outside our lives. "What about the gambling fronts?" I asked, conscious of how integral they were to our family business and their connections.

"The gambling operations are tied into the drug routes as well—a hidden network of money laundering that keeps us afloat." His fingers danced over the keyboard, pulling up additional information. "If we can expose any weaknesses in their operations, it could give us leverage."

I narrowed my eyes at the screen, my thoughts racing. "We have to bolster our security in both areas. If Giovanni senses any hint of weakness, he'll pounce. We cannot allow that."

"Agreed," Dante nodded, the determination in his eyes mirroring my own. "I've already reached out to Gino and

Marco to assess the security around our gambling operations. We need to expand our protective measures, both on the streets and inside our establishments."

"We also need to adopt new protocols," I suggested, my heart racing at the possibilities. "Educate our staff on recognizing suspicious activity, and invest in technology to monitor operations more closely. We can't afford to miss a single detail."

"Definitely," Dante replied, looking energized by the ideas swirling around us. "We'll implement training for our employees, starting with the gambling fronts. Anyone connected to the drug routes must be scrutinized."

The urgency between us ignited a fire in my chest, and I felt empowered in our shared mission. It wasn't just about survival; it was about taking control of our narrative. We had to ensure that our family, our legacy, stood unyielding against Giovanni's threats.

"Let's also reach out to our allies," I proposed. "We need their support as we fortify our positions. If we can leverage their networks, it may help to deter Giovanni's advances."

"Absolutely." Dante beamed, his enthusiasm infectious. "I can set up a meeting with the Mancinis and others who have been loyal to us. If we unite our strengths, we can send a clear message."

As plans began to take shape, the gravity of our situation settled in. Giovanni had mastered the art of manipulation, and his underhanded tactics threatened to unravel everything we had cultivated. The tangled web of drug routes and gambling operations was integral to our family business; if we lost that, we could find ourselves vulnerable, our foundation crumbling beneath us.

Walking through the kitchen, I allowed myself a moment of vulnerability as I leaned against the counter. "Dante, it scares me to think what could happen if Giovanni gets a foothold in our territory. This isn't just about business; it's about our lives and our growing family."

Dante stepped close, softening as he spoke, "I know, Alessia. But we cannot let fear control our actions. The moment we show weakness is the moment he'll exploit us. But we both know, even as we keep news of our baby private to the family, word will get out. It always does with things like this."

His words soothed the storm swelling inside me, and I found reassurance in the strength radiating from him. "You're right. He will see the baby as both our weakest point and a threat, as the next generation of our family legacy is here." I straighten my back. "We'll do this together, and we'll be proactive."

A determined look crossed Dante's face. "Let's outline the steps we need to take. I want you involved in every aspect of this."

We spent the next hour compiling strategies, drafting contingency plans for securing our operations and addressing vulnerabilities in both our gambling fronts and drug routes. There was something soothing about the rhythm of our collaboration, the way our minds were in sync as we worked through the complexities together.

But just then, a thought crept in—what if it wasn't enough? Giovanni's ambition was becoming clearer. His true colors were coming out, and he was becoming like his father— unrelenting, subtle, and quiet in his tactics. As I worked through the implications of our strategies, the knot of anxiety tightened within me again.

"What happens if Giovanni retaliates before we're prepared?" I asked, my voice trembling slightly.

"We'll be ready," Dante assured, but I could sense the weight of uncertainty in his tone. He was protective, yet I knew there was a part of him wrestling with fear as well. If Giovanni sensed weakness or distraction, he would strike deeper into our territory, daring us to start a war with so much now at stake. And any plans for deepening our empire and strengthening our influence could be upended in an instant.

"Remember how like a shadow he was at the charity gala? He wears a mask of quiet, of calm control. As if he wants to be overlooked and dismissed by his enemies. But I get the feeling there is a monster awakening within him. We can't underestimate him," I pressed, my mind racing. "His tactics are like his father's, ruthless, and their family has shown they'll stop at nothing to exploit vulnerabilities. If he catches wind of our preparations… I can't imagine the lengths he'll go to."

Dante caught my gaze, his expression sharpening. "Then we can't allow him to gain that information. We need to keep everything under wraps, operating from a position of stealth. If anyone senses our anxiety, it could sink our plans."

The reality of his words sent a chill down my spine. The stakes were perilously high, and the tension between us amplified, intertwining our fates in a way that felt both exhilarating and dangerous.

I leaned forward, meeting his eyes with conviction. "We'll remain vigilant and precise in our actions—all the while projecting strength. We can do this, Dante. Together, we'll rise against Giovanni and protect our family."

His lips curled into a smile, and for a moment, the tension in the air eased. "Yes, together. We'll unite our defenses, bolster our operations, and push back against every threat that comes our way. Giovanni won't know what hit him."

As the evening unfolded, I could feel the bubbling energy between us, a deep sense of purpose igniting our shared vision. The road ahead would undoubtedly be filled with challenges, but I remained steadfast in my determination to carve out a path where our family wouldn't just survive but thrive.

If we were to fortify our defenses against the drug routes and gambling businesses, and reclaim every inch of the territory that was ours by right, we would emerge victorious, together. Giovanni may have chaos and ambition at his disposal, but we had love, loyalty, and a fierce fire that could not be extinguished.

The weight of the world hung heavy, and reality was far from simple. But as I stood beside Dante, I knew that together, we could brave this storm and rise above the challenges, stronger than ever before. Every gamble we took now would shape the future of our family, and I was ready to face the consequences head-on.

Chapter 9: A Dangerous Game - Alessia's POV

The shadows shifted around me as I made my way through the dimly lit halls of the Moretti estate, my heart racing with a mix of anticipation and anxiety. Tonight was pivotal as Dante had doubled the number of men patrolling the borders of our territory. He had paired loyal men with those he was not sure he could trust—if there were traitors in our midst, they would be sussed out.

I felt as if the very walls of the family estate were closing in, echoing with whispers of long-buried secrets and hidden agendas. My determination to explore the depths of Dante's family's dealings drove me forward, a fierce desire to uncover the truth before we found ourselves ensnared by Giovanni's ambitions. I wasn't sure what I was looking for, only that I was part of this family now, and I needed to do my part to keep us safe. I couldn't roam the streets and face our enemies there, so I would do the next best thing, there, in the estate.

After the recent family meeting, I couldn't shake the feeling that something deeper lurked beneath the surface of our reality, an unsettling sensation that the delicate balance of power among our families was on the brink of upheaval. My instinct told me that there was more at play than just the gambling enterprises and drug routes—the business dealings we'd been focused on.

As I entered Dante's father's study, the air was thick with the scent of aged wood and leather-bound books. A rich tapestry of our family's history adorned the walls, but they also concealed the shadows of betrayal and ambition. "I need to find something," I whispered to myself, calculating where to start. "Anything that could help us stop Giovanni without resorting to violence."

My fingers brushed over the intricate wood paneling of the file cabinets, and I began rifling through the documents piled carefully within. I had always been curious about the inner workings of our family, but now that curiosity felt urgent, even necessary. I wanted to understand the precise dynamics at play—the alliances, the rivalries, the questionable players in this dangerous game, and the pathways that dictated our survival in a world fraught with danger.

After a few frustrating moments of searching, I stumbled across a folder labeled "Rivetti Negotiations." Giovanni's family file. My heart quickened as I pulled it free, settling into the leather chair at the desk. Inside, I found a series of documents, correspondence, and meeting notes that revealed a web of alliances I had never previously explored.

As I thumbed through the papers, I felt a knot form in my stomach—a chilling sensation that these revelations could significantly alter the ongoing conflict between our families. The correspondence suggested that Giovanni was not merely attempting to disrupt our operations; he was forging alliances with families who had traditionally remained neutral. The implications began to dawn on me like a rising tide, threatening to sweep away the stability we had fought so hard to maintain.

One document caught my eye, a memo detailing meetings between Rivetti and an unidentified female who was driving a Mancini car. The Mancinis were a family we had closely aligned with. Elena was a friend of mine, socially speaking, though, not personally. My heart sank as I absorbed the information. It was clear: Giovanni was strategically manipulating someone in the Mancini family, attempting to steer them toward an alliance that could drastically shift the balance of power away from us.

If the Mancinis sided with Giovanni, it would not only bolster his influence but also rob us of our most significant ally. I felt a surge of panic as images of a destabilized future flickered through my mind, a cascading effect that could undermine everything our family had worked for.

Rubbing my temples, I tried to think despite the panic swirling within me. What could I do with this information? How could I present it to Dante and the others in a way that would prevent us from losing everything?

Suddenly, a disturbing realization washed over me—if Giovanni pursued this alliance, he might also leverage it to intimidate others, creating a network that could suffocate our operations. The interconnectedness of our lives began to feel like an intricate game of chess, with every piece capable of tipping the scales toward disaster.

The meeting notes reflected discussions of lucrative joint ventures into new gambling markets, and my eyes widened as I continued to read. Not only were they discussing drug routes, but they were also planning to divvy up the territories that had long been considered ours. Giovanni's strategy was one of a master manipulator, and I shivered at the crafty nature of his maneuvering.

I leaned back in my chair, savoring the gravity of the information I had uncovered. The danger was palpable; we were facing something far more disruptive than I had originally anticipated. While I had initially focused on securing our operations and reinforcing alliances, Giovanni's efforts indicated that he was prepared to wage an expansive war—one that included financial and territorial seizures.

A surge of anger ignited within me, swirling and building. I had to act quickly and decisively before the weight of this information risked our future. My instincts screamed that time was running out, and I couldn't waste a second.

With shaky hands, I gathered the documents, organizing them into a neat pile. I knew I couldn't sit idly by; I had to bring this to Dante's attention immediately. We needed to forge a strategy that would counter Giovanni's deceit before it solidified into something irreversible.

I rushed out of the study, my heart pounding against my ribcage as I made my way down the hall toward Dante's office. The urgency pulsed through my veins, propelling me forward. I burst into his office, finding him leaning over papers strewn across the desk. The intensity in his gaze as he glanced up was met with surprise.

"Alessia! What's wrong?" His immediate concern soothed part of my racing heart.

"I found something," I said breathlessly, sweeping the documents onto the desk. "You need to see this."

Dante's brows furrowed in concentration as he examined the papers, his expression shifting from curiosity to apprehension. "What exactly am I looking at?"

I took a deep breath, steeling myself as I explained. "These documents detail Giovanni's discussions with someone wearing a hat and sunglasses—one of the women in the Mancini family. He's trying to form an alliance that could change the entire power dynamics of our families. If they band together, it'll leave us vulnerable."

Dante's eyes widened as he absorbed the implications, the tension in the air thickening. "Is it Elena?"

I shrug slowly. "I don't think so. But her father is one of seven in his family. The list of her cousins is vast, Dante."

"This is worse than I thought. The Mancinis have been loyal to us."

"They've been discussing plans that involve drug routes and joint ventures into new gambling territories," I continued, urgency lacing my words. "If they cement this alliance, Giovanni will gain the upper hand, and we'll be left scrambling for influence."

A scowl crossed Dante's face, his determination surging through the air like a storm. "We can't let this happen. We need to approach the Mancinis before they become entrenched in this alliance. We have to make clear the stakes and the consequences of siding with Giovanni."

"Exactly," I agreed, feeling a renewed sense of hope as we began to strategize together. "We need to remind them of the loyalty we've shared and the dangers of aligning with someone like Giovanni. They must understand that he cannot be trusted."

Dante nodded, his gaze blazing with intensity. "We'll gather a team and prepare our arguments. If we present this properly, we may be able to sway them before it's too late. But time is of the essence. We need to act now."

As we laid out our plan, outlining our approach to the Mancinis, I felt the gravity of our situation settle in—a dangerous game of moves and counter moves. My earlier fears transformed into a focused energy that filled me with purpose and determination. We were not only fighting for our family's legacy; we were fighting for the future of our child—a new generation that didn't have to navigate the same dark waters we had been thrust into.

We spent hours poring over the nuances of our strategy, relentlessly preparing for what lay ahead. The more we dissected the information I had found, the more resolute I became—this was our fight, one that we would not lose.

Marco knocked once and then entered the room. "You called for me, boss?"

I gracefully stood, making my exit. This conversation about Elena was one I would not partake in. They would discuss it, man to man. I hoped for all our sakes that Elena was not involved.

As the sun dipped below the horizon, I felt a shift within me, an unyielding fire igniting—our family and our future were worth defending at all costs. I would not allow Giovanni to rob our child of their legacy, nor would I stand idly by as our family fell apart.

With the pieces now in motion, I felt a surge of empowerment course through my veins. We would confront Giovanni's dark schemes head-on and prove that our love and loyalty would always eclipse the shadows threatening to obscure our future.

Together, we would rise from the chaos and reshape our narrative. The game of power had begun, and I was ready to play.

Chapter 10: Fragile Trust - Marco's POV

The city hummed below my windows, neon lights throwing long shadows across the floor of my loft. Midnight clung to the skyline, thick and silent. I leaned against the glass, arms folded, watching for her. When the elevator chimed and the soft pad of footsteps crossed the threshold, I already knew it's her.

"Elena," I said, my voice low.

She was wearing black—tight jeans, fitted jacket, hair pulled back. Her face was unreadable, but her eyes... her eyes always gave her away. There was tension in them. And something else. Guilt? I tried not to jump to it.

"You said it couldn't wait," she said.

I nodded. "It can't."

She closed the door behind her and walked in slow, every movement graceful. Controlled. That's the thing about Elena Mancini—she was raised in chaos, but she learned to carry herself like royalty.

I kept my distance for now. "Giovanni Rivetti met with someone three nights ago. A woman. Disguised. Drove a Mancini car."

Her brow twitched, cheeks flushed. "You think it was me?"

I stared at her, searching her face. "I need to hear it from you."

Elena drew in a sharp breath, beautiful face looking hurt. "No, Marco. It wasn't me. I haven't seen Rivetti since the charity gala at the Morettis. Not once."

"You're sure?"

Her hands balled into fists at her sides. "Yes. I don't know who it was."

"It was a woman," I said carefully, stepping closer to the woman who is fast owning my heart.

She shook her head. "Not from my family. Staff, maybe? No one's said anything. But... the car, the disguise... it's got to be someone close."

I watched her jaw tighten. This world she was born into—it eats people alive. It has a way of turning blood cold and loyalty into a coin that flips too easily.

"Why would someone from the Mancinis meet with Rivetti?" I asked.

Her voice cracked a little when she answers, "I don't know. Maybe they're tired of living on the edge. Maybe they're trying to do more than survive."

I stepped closer, arms wrapping around her, though I knew I should keep my distance until I'm sure she was telling me the truth. "And you?"

She looked up at me. "What about me?"

"Are you tired of it too?"

Her mouth opened, then closed. "I don't know anymore, Marco. I'm chasing a life that doesn't exist in our world. I want something... normal. Real. But every time I try to walk away, something like this pulls me back in. Secrets. Betrayals. Men with guns in the dark. It's always the same."

She turned her face slightly, and I saw the flicker of tears she fought to hide.

I closed the space between us, her body flush to mine. One hand on her cheek, the other at her waist. "You didn't do this," I said, more to myself than her. "I believe you."

She lifted her eyes to mine. "Then why does it still feel like I'm the enemy?"

I pulled her face to me, no more words. I kissed her hard, because she needed to feel it—the loyalty, the heat, the devotion. It wasn't just about protecting her. It was about choosing her. Every time.

Her hands gripped my shirt. Her breath was fire against my mouth. When we finally pulled apart, I pressed my forehead to hers.

"I'm going to take care of this," I whispered. "I'll find out who it was."

"And if it's someone I love? Family?" she asked softly.

"Then we deal with it. Together."

***

Dante's estate was quiet this late. The lights were low, the staff invisible, and the walls held more secrets than the city outside ever would. I found him in the sitting room, sipping bourbon, a book open in his lap but unread.

He didn't look up when I entered. "Did you speak with her?"

I nodded once. "I did."

"And?"

"She says she didn't meet with Rivetti. Swears it."

He finally lifted his gaze to mine. "And you believe her?"

I walked closer, standing across from him. "Yes."

"Why?"

"Because I know her. I know what it looks like when she lies. And I know what it looks like when someone's hurting."

Dante's jaw clenched. "This isn't a game, Marco. If she's playing us—"

"She's not."

He stood, slower than usual, but with purpose. "Then who met with Rivetti?"

"I don't know yet. But I'm starting to think it was someone trying to frame the Mancinis." I crossed my muscled arms. "Elena hasn't heard anything from the staff or the family about this meeting."

His eyes narrowed. "I don't like unknowns."

"Neither do I."

He studied me, that cold silence he uses to measure loyalty. Then he said, "Why should I trust your word on this?"

I stared back, no hesitation. "Same reason you trust my hands with your business. Same reason you trust me to walk into the fire for you. Because we're in this together. Same family. Same code."

He looked away, just for a second. That's the crack. The weight he carried—it's not just power. It's knowing betrayal comes from the inside more than the outside.

Finally, he exhaled. "Find the truth. Fast."

"I will."

I turned to go, but he called out, "Marco."

I paused in the doorway.

"If you're wrong about her..."

"I'm not," I said.

And I left it at that.

Chapter 11: The Ultimatum - Alessia's POV

The penthouse loomed like a bastion above the bustling streets of New York, a fortress gilded in luxury but tinged with shadows. Standing in the living room, the grandiose décor of dark mahogany and plush velvet spoke of power and wealth, yet tonight it felt suffocating—heavy with the weight of unspoken secrets and the tension that crackled in the air like static.

I looked out the floor-to-ceiling windows, the city glowing beneath a canopy of stars, each twinkling light a reminder of the vibrant life outside, a stark contrast to the uncertainty within these walls. Everything felt like a game of chess, and the players were not just my family but rival factions that lay in wait, ready to pounce at the first sign of weakness.

Tonight was crucial. Giovanni Rivetti had played his hand, and the ultimatum he'd laid at Dante's feet had thrown our world into disarray. My heart beat heavily in my chest as I replayed the conversation Dante had shared with me earlier. Giovanni's demand had felt more like a dagger aimed at the heart of our family—an attempt to tear apart the very fabric we had woven together.

"Alessia!" Dante called from the adjoining room, breaking me from my reverie. His voice was tense, laced with urgency. "We need to talk."

I turned swiftly, gathering the courage to meet whatever news he had for me. Fear settled in my stomach, coiling like a snake, ready to strike. I stepped into the room, drawn to him like a moth to a flame. His face was resolute, but I could see the storms raging behind his hazel eyes.

"Sit," he instructed, pulling a chair out for me at the round table in the center of the dining room. The table felt like a battleground, polished and scarred from years of discussions that shaped our family's fate. I knew this conversation held the potential to change everything.

"What did Giovanni say?" I asked, fear creeping into my voice as I took a seat. I needed to hear it directly from him— the implications of Giovanni's ultimatum could upend our lives.

"He wants us to surrender some territory," Dante said, running a hand through his hair, a gesture that betrayed his frustration. "He's leveraging our past dealings to control our future, and it's going to make our lives even more complicated. He has allies he believes will back him up."

My stomach twisted at the revelation. Territory wasn't merely about land; it was about power, influence, reputation. Giovanni was playing a dangerous game, one that could potentially unravel every alliance we had.

"What are our options?" I pressed, needing to know how we could navigate this treacherous landscape.

"We need to make a decision soon," he replied. "If we refuse, he will retaliate. We cannot let our enemies see us as vulnerable."

I could feel the weight of his words settle like a shroud between us, casting a shadow over our hopes. "How many men does he have?" I asked, trying to assess the threat level, to understand the battleground. This wasn't just about our family anymore; this was a war of wills, a contest for supremacy.

"Too many," Dante said, his brows furrowing in thought. "I estimate at least twice our number. But it's not just about strength in numbers. Giovanni thrives on deception and fear."

"Do we know who he's allied with?" I probed further, needing to understand the intricate web Giovanni wove around himself. This was about survival; we had to know our enemies to defend our territory effectively.

"He's tied in with the Genovese family. If they back him, it will spell trouble for us," he replied, his voice filled with concern. "They'll want to leverage our vulnerabilities."

"Does anyone support us?" My heart ached at the thought that we might be standing alone against a tide of adversaries. The fear of betrayal lurked just beneath the surface, whispering doubts that threatened to churn my resolve.

"Gino and the Mancini crew might stand with us, but we need to solidify those alliances before we make any moves," he said, determination creeping back into his voice. "Tonight, we'll reach out and shore up our defenses."

Dante's steadfastness invigorated me, but I felt the burden of our choices sink into my bones. "What if we go to the meeting he requested?" I suggested, my mind racing with possibilities. "If we show willingness to negotiate, we might buy time. We can gather more information and see what he's really planning."

He considered my words, then nodded slowly. "That could work, but I need to know you'll stay safe. I can't risk losing you, especially not now."

A pang of fear spiked through my heart, but I pushed it down, determination flaring instead. "Dante, I am not going to let fear dictate my actions. We're in this together, remember?"

He reached out, his fingers brushing against my hand, igniting a spark between us. "I know. But I need you to promise me you'll be careful. Giovanni is cunning; he'll use every trick in the book."

"I promise," I replied softly, locking my gaze with his. This was our fight. We would face it together, head-on.

The weight of our conversation hung heavy in the air as we strategized our next steps. Beneath the surface of our discussions lay the knowledge of the dark underbelly of our world. The murky dealings, the whispered conversations, and the covert operations that thrived in the shadows—they were all just a breath away, and one misstep could spell doom for us.

As we continued to plan, I felt a rush of emotions—fear, love, determination—a cocktail that defined our reality as members of this world. We were entrenched in this life of loyalty and violence, and I had accepted that the secrets which surrounded us were just as alive as the men controlling them.

A sudden knock at the door jolted me from my thoughts, reverberating through the tense atmosphere like a gunshot. Dante tensed, his expression sharpening, and I knew the moment to act had arrived.

"Stay here," he instructed, stepping toward the door.

I felt the familiar instinct to argue, to remind him of my place at his side, but the urgency in his eyes silenced my protests. This was his role, his burden to bear.

The door swung open, revealing Marco, his face taut, a mixture of anxiety and determination etched into his features. "We need to talk," he announced, urgency flooding his voice. "Things are moving faster than we expected."

"What do you mean?" I asked, stepping closer, needing to glean whatever information he was bringing into the room.

"Giovanni has sent word to several families—he's trying to stir up doubt among our allies. We need to act now before it's too late," Marco replied, scanning the room. "I can't shake the feeling that he's preparing for something big."

"What do you suggest?" Dante asked, lingering on the edge of tension, ready to lead us through the storm.

"Let's gather the family and the crews tonight," Marco suggested. "We can confront them together and stand united against whatever Giovanni has planned."

The weight of his words struck a chord deep within me. Unity was our strongest weapon, and it felt like a promising strategy. "We'll call Gino and the others," I said, bolstered by their support. "But we must prepare for his retaliation. If Giovanni thinks he can divide us, he will discover just how wrong he is."

Dante nodded, a glimmer of admiration shining in his eyes. "We'll show them that the Moretti family is not to be trifled with. Together, we're unshakable."

As plans began to take shape, I could feel fear and uncertainty seep into the corners of my mind once more. But alongside it was a fierce determination; the stakes had never been higher, and our resolve was palpable.

The shadows of secrets grew in the corners of the penthouse as we strategized, weaving plans to counter Giovanni's impending onslaught. The night around us hummed with the anticipation of what lay ahead—a reckoning that would shake the very foundation of our family, but we would face it head-on.

Together, we held the power to rewrite not only our future but that of the families bound to us. This was our legacy, interwoven with shadows and secrets, whispering promises of strength and loyalty enshrined in blood. There would be no backing down; we would emerge more united than ever, determined to guard our territory against anyone who dared to challenge us.

As I looked into Dante's eyes, I felt the fire of our resolve ignite, a promise that no ultimatum could extinguish. The time had come to reclaim our power, to stand tall against those who dared to threaten our family. Giovanni may have drawn the lines, but we would write the story—one drenched in loyalty, honor, and the unbreakable spirit of the Moretti name.

Chapter 12: Betrayal - Dante's POV

The wind howled outside the penthouse, sending a shiver through me as I trudged across the polished marble floor. Shadows danced around the edges of the room, growing longer as evening descended upon the city.

With every step I took, the weight of my thoughts pressed down on me like a tangible force. Remembering the new revelations about Giovanni's maneuvering kept the embers of anger alive within me, flickering dangerously close to rage.

Alessia's discovery about the impending alliance between Giovanni and someone in the Mancini family had fueled our urgency and laid bare the vulnerabilities in our family's position.

The Mancini patriarch had insisted he knew nothing of who had taken one of the family's cars to meet with Giovanni, but he had proposed that it could be a staff member, not one of the family.

Too many mysteries for my comfort. The mere thought of them teaming up was unsettling—it threatened not only our dominance in the drug routes but could create a rivalry that would see us squeezed from both ends. But even worse than the threat from outside was the realization that our family had been infiltrated from within.

I stood by the window, looking out over the vast sprawl of New York City, calculating just how much was at stake. My mind was a whirlwind of concerns—how could we protect our family? What steps would we need to take? And then the most daunting question of all: who could I trust?

The uncertainty gnawed at me, forcing me to confront dangers lurking closer to home. It was during a recent meeting, one that had been shrouded in secrecy, that I discovered the truth—a betrayal that pierced deep into the heart of our family.

My thoughts returned to that rainy night a few days prior, when I had convened a meeting with Gino and Marco, hoping to strengthen our defenses against Giovanni's threats. As we gathered around a table laden with papers, the atmosphere had been thick with tension, every man acutely aware of the stakes we faced. We had spent the night discussing strategies while the rain lashed against the windows, a fitting accompaniment for the dark cloud settling over us.

At that meeting, as plans were being finalized, I noticed Gino's demeanor change. He had hesitated when I asked him about certain discrepancies in our supply lines and evasions in our security protocols—little cracks appearing in our careful façade. It seemed as if he stumbled over his words, an uneasy tension creeping into his posture as he tried to articulate the hidden issues we had barely scratched the surface of.

"Dante, I…" Gino began, his voice trailing off, but the look in his eyes was enough to know something was amiss. It wasn't just angling for protection; it felt as if he was being torn in two, a contradiction of loyalty battling against a wave of unseen pressures.

"Don't," I said, cutting him off. "This is serious. If there's something you're not telling me, now is the time. We can't afford secrets between us."

The silence hung heavily in the air, a taut string ready to snap, and Marco shared a concerned glance with me, nodding in agreement.

Finally, Gino exhaled sharply, as if steeling himself for a confession. "There have been whispers... rumors about a leak.

Someone within our personal ranks has been passing information to Giovanni."

Rage flared in my chest at the mention of our enemy's name, but I contained it, desperate for clarity. Leaks in our outer ranks were normal, usually born from rumor or gossip, but leaks from within the inner circle were not to be tolerated.

"Do you have any idea who? We need to handle this before it blows up in our faces."

He nodded slowly, his jaw clenched. "I suspect it might be someone close to us—someone who has access to our operations. Some of the new recruits in the family might be involved, connections we haven't fully vetted."

Those words sent a chill through my spine. The idea that someone inside our family could betray us was insidious, rising like a serpent coiling around my heart. We couldn't risk it. I cast my mind back over recent recruits, friends, and associates we had brought in to strengthen our network.

"Gino, we need names—now," I urged, digging deep into the memory of our dealings. The weight of responsibility settled on me like a heavy cloak. If Giovanni was pooling intelligence to undermine us, we had to act swiftly.

Later that night, the sense of dread was palpable as Gino and Marco provided me with what little information they had gleaned. We discussed names, scrutinizing every recent recruit and associates who had exhibited suspicious behavior. The conversations crackled with tension, each name I heard stoking a fire of indignation within me. I felt betrayed.

It was during one of these discussions that Marco finally brought up a name that sent my heart racing—Antonio. He had always been among the more charismatic members of our circle, an affable confidant who had spent years alongside us. His charm masked a cunning disposition, one I had overlooked in a world fraught with threats.

"I saw him whispering to one of Giovanni's men at Mario's tavern last week," Marco said, his brows furrowed in concern. "They were too close for comfort, and it didn't sit right with me." He paused. "Rumor has it that he is mentoring Luca."

"Speak with Luca immediately. Remind him where his loyalty lies." Luca was an upbeat and young member of our family, easily influenced by a seasoned man like Antonio.

My stomach turned at the thought of Antonio's possible betrayal. He was more than just a business partner; he had been a trusted friend, one of the men I had fought with at my side. I couldn't fathom that he would betray everything we had built together.

"What's his motive?" I wondered aloud, searching for understanding amidst the chaos.

"That's the thing," Gino replied, his voice losing some of its steadiness. "He's been struggling to keep his own businesses afloat. Rumors suggest he's been entangled with some of the riskier ventures in the gambling sector, and if Giovanni's offering a lifeline, it might be enough to sway him."

Anger flared hot in my chest, just beneath the surface. "A lifeline? He's risking our entire family for an alliance that's as volatile as the drugs we're dealing with? He's courting a disaster!"

"We need to confront him," Marco said, his concern matched only by determination. "If we let this fester, it will only grow worse. We should schedule a meeting to gauge his loyalty—to see if there's any truth to the suspicions."

My mind was already racing, weighed down by the implications of facing a man I once considered family. To confront Antonio would not only expose potential betrayal; it could further complicate relationships, spilling secrets that could tear our lives apart even further.

"Fine, we'll set a meeting," I conceded, steeling myself for the confrontation. "But we go prepared. We need to make it clear that any alliance with Giovanni will not be tolerated. We'll give him a choice—stand with us or stand against us."

In that moment, as plans took form, I felt a surge of energy coursing through me. We were up against a deadly game; and the fate of our family hung in the balance. I would not allow betrayal to tear us down.

The following day, as the early morning sun crept into the penthouse, I could barely contain my anxiety. Each tick of the clock felt like a countdown, amplifying my resolve to weather the storm looming ahead. I needed to confront Antonio before Giovanni's influence snuffed out everything we had built.

When Antonio finally arrived, I stood with Gino and Marco in the dining room, tension thickening the air around us. He walked through the door with his characteristic confidence, but I could sense a shadow of uncertainty that only heightened my resolve.

"Dante! Gino! Marco!" he greeted with a wide grin, but I noticed it was laced with an undercurrent of bravado. "What's the occasion?"

"It's about time we had a conversation, Antonio. You have been spending too much time with Giovanni's men," I stated boldly, cutting through the pleasantries.

His expression shifted slightly, tension flickering in his eyes. "What do you mean? This is all a misunderstanding. We have nothing to worry about."

"Don't we?" I challenged, the fire of anger rising in my chest again. "The rumors of you visiting Mario's tavern, speaking to Giovanni—those are not misunderstandings. You know what's at stake for our family."

He cleared his throat, his confidence wavering. "I'm merely keeping my options open. Business is—"

"Business?" I interrupted, my voice rising. "By aligning yourself with our enemy you are risking everything we've built. You're risking our lives, Antonio. What's left of our family?"

In that moment, the tension thickened, and I caught a glimpse of the turmoil in his dark eyes. The man I had once trusted stood before me at a precipice, and I couldn't fathom what was driving him to betray our family.

"I need this, Dante," he shouted back, desperation creeping into his voice. "The industry is changing; the landscape is tougher. If I align myself with Giovanni, I might salvage my business."

"And in doing so, you would undermine our entire operation," I shot back, anger flooding my veins. "You don't realize he's playing you for a fool, right? He would throw you under the bus without hesitation!"

As tensions flared surrounding us like a tempest, I could see his resolve wavering. "But what choice do I have? I can't just sit back while everything crumbles around me."

"If you stand with Giovanni now, everything will crumble. You'll lead us all to ruin," I said, my voice steadying, even as anger twisted inside of me. "You're risking our family for a false sense of security."

Antonio's gaze flitted to Marco and Gino, who stood nearby, ready to support whatever choice I deemed necessary. Their eyes held stern determination as they bore witness to the tension unfolding.

"Choose wisely, Antonio," Gino warned, his tone low and measured. "You have a chance to step back from this brink of betrayal."

"It's not too late to reconsider," Marco added, his expression unwavering. "Stand with us. Fight for our family. Fight for what matters."

The silence in the room became deafening as I held my breath, waiting for Antonio's response. I could feel the heaviness of the moment settle over us, pressing down like a weight that threatened to crush everything.

Finally, Antonio's shoulders slumped, betrayal lingering in the air like a poison between us. "I… I need to think."

With that, he turned to leave, the resignation in his voice echoing through the room as he walked out. Betrayal had pierced the heart of our family, leaving us teetering on the brink of devastation.

As the door clicked shut behind him, I felt a void grow where friendship had once thrived. I could almost hear the delicate threads of loyalty fraying, the raw wound of betrayal laid bare.

We were wading into dangerous waters, and the fire of retribution was now set to burn brightly within me. Giovanni's edges inched closer, but now a deeper wound lingered among us—one that could potentially disrupt everything.

Time was running out, and there was no room for doubts. As the shadows lengthened, I felt the depths of desperation swell within me, fueling my resolve to protect what mattered most. The fight was far from over, and I would not rest until our family emerged from this storm, reborn and stronger than ever before.

Chapter 13: A Shattered Alliance - Alessia's POV

The streets of New York, always alive with noise and energy, felt particularly frenetic tonight. I walked through the dimly lit corridors of the penthouse, my nerves fraying as shadows flickered along the walls, reflecting the turmoil gripping my heart. The tension that had begun to brew earlier this week now simmered dangerously close to boiling over. The discovery of betrayal within our ranks had shaken the very foundation of our family.

Dante had remained adamant about tackling the potential alliance between the Mancinis and Giovanni, but the weight of uncertainty pressed heavily upon us. I could feel the fissures forming in our family, like cracks in a dam on the verge of collapse. Every word exchanged, every glance shared, seemed to pulsate with unspoken doubts, and I feared for what was to come.

As I approached the living area, I noticed Dante and Gino deep in conversation, their voices low but urgent. The gravity etched in their expressions sent a rush of apprehension coursing through me. "What's going on?" I interrupted, stepping forward.

Dante looked up, his brow furrowing as he glanced at Gino. "We might have a bigger problem than we thought," he said, taking a deep breath. "There are whispers that Luca is in talks with Giovanni. He's been seen meeting with some of Giovanni's men."

"What?" My stomach tightened at the very mention of Luca's name. "Luca would never betray us like that. He's family!"

"Family can betray too," Gino replied grimly, his voice steady. "If he's entangled with Giovanni, it changes everything. We stand to lose our position."

"Loyalty is a fickle thing," Dante added, his gaze serious. "And it's clear Giovanni is trying to capitalize on any weakness he can find."

Just as I was about to respond, the front door swung open, and Marco entered. I immediately sensed an unusual tension surrounding him, an air of guilt clinging to his presence as he stepped into the room. I knew there was something weighing heavily on his shoulders, but with everything happening, I didn't know if I had the strength to deal with yet another revelation.

"Marco," I greeted, my voice taut with anticipation. "We need to know what's going on. Do you know anything about Luca?"

He met my gaze, his expression shifting from defiance to something softer, and I caught a glimpse of uncertainty. "I've heard some things." Marco hesitated, searching for the right words. "But it's complicated."

"Complicated?" I echoed, frustration bubbling within me. "This isn't the time for vague explanations. Lives are at stake. We can't afford to tiptoe around the truth any longer."

Marco met my piercing gaze, his brow furrowing as he took a deep breath. "Fine. I've heard rumors about Luca's discussions with Giovanni, but there's something else—but I don't know how to say it."

"Just say it!" Dante urged, tension coiling in the air around us.

"Rumor has it," Marco began, his voice shaky, "that there's a connection between Giovanni and my late mother, Lucia.

They had an affair years ago. Right before Pops… well, before he walked out with his mistress. It's possible that—"

"What are you implying?" I cut in, unable to comprehend the weight of his words. My heart raced, dread pooling in my stomach as I felt time standing still.

"Marco, are you saying you could be…?" Gino began, trailing off in disbelief.

The truth hung in the air like a lead weight. "I'm saying that there's a chance Giovanni is my father," Marco confessed, his voice trembling with the admission. "I only started putting the pieces together recently, but if it's true, it complicates everything."

The shock of his words sent a tremor through my body, and I could barely catch my breath. How could everything I thought I knew about Marco collapse so swiftly? My closest friend—and possibly, the son of the man who is fast becoming our greatest enemy.

"Your mother was with Giovanni?" I breathed, trying to process this new reality that turned everything upside down. "How could she keep this from us? How could you not know before now?"

"I found an old letter when I was cleaning out the old family trunks," Marco confessed, his voice heavy with emotion. "One of her journals mentioned Giovanni, how he promised her the world. I've always known there was something she wasn't telling me, something about him that kept her so guarded."

Dante's gaze shifted from Marco to me, his thoughts racing as the implications sank in. "This changes everything. Not only is Luca possibly betraying us, but Giovanni has an inside connection with you, Marco. He could use that against us."

Marco's expression hardened, but I could see the turmoil swirling behind his eyes. "I never wanted this. I don't want to be part of Giovanni's world."

The complexity of the situation left my mind reeling. The thin strands of trust that bound our families together now felt all too fragile. Everyone was at risk—friends and foes mingled with no certainty of where loyalties lay.

"What do we do?" I asked, my voice barely above a whisper, overwhelmed by the confluence of betrayal and confusion. "We can't let Giovanni manipulate this situation. If he uses your lineage, Marco, he could destroy us from within."

"I will not let that happen," Marco replied firmly, his resolve igniting in the uncertainty. "We must confront Luca and gain the boy's loyalty back. He holds more than just information about Giovanni; he holds the loyalty of our friends, too."

"Confronting him will not be easy," I warned, my heart pounding against my chest. "He may see this as treason and retaliate. We can't let him know we're aware of his plans."

As the three of us gathered closer, our sense of determination strengthened. Gut feelings gave way to the realization that we must act decisively. There was no room for hesitation.

"Let's organize a meeting," I suggested, gathering my thoughts. "We can use the strength of our family ties while protecting the integrity of our operations. Perhaps if we present a united front, we can remind Luca where his true loyalties lie."

Dante nodded, his brow furrowing as he moved back to his earlier resolve. "We have to gauge where everyone stands. If Luca is indeed in league with Giovanni, then we need to prepare for the worst."

As we began to devise our strategy, I could feel the weight of what lay ahead—an impending confrontation charged with uncertainty and risk. Betrayal lingered like a specter, cloaked in shadows and deception—it threatened to consume us.

Minutes turned into hours as we planned our approach, carefully crafting our messaging to secure the loyalty of those we could trust within our ranks. My emotions churned within me, an unpredictable storm brewing among the remnants of shattered trust. The echo of Marco's potential parentage lurked in the back of my mind, an unsettling reminder of how deeply betrayal could cut.

To confront Luca was one thing, but now I wondered about how deep Giovanni's influence reached—not just within our operations, but among us, interwoven in our lives and relationships. What would happen if the web of deceit continued to unravel?

"Stay resolute," I urged as we gathered our final notes and strategies. "Together, we'll counteract Giovanni's moves with our own. We're stronger together, and if we present unity, there's no way we won't succeed."

Dante's eyes met mine, determination lighting a fire deep within. In the depths of my heart, I hoped we would unearth the truth, confront the impending threat, and emerge not only unscathed but united against the chaos drawing near.

As the evening drew on and plans solidified, my resolve deepened. I could handle the upheaval, however troubling. We were still the Morettis, bound by blood, loyalty, and purpose. Together, we would not only face the impending storm but defy the currents threatening to pull us under.

In the daunting silence of the night, I prepared myself for the battles ahead, knowing that navigating the complexities of betrayal would take not just strength but strategy—and that amidst all the turmoil, hope still flickered, casting a beacon toward a brighter future.

Chapter 14: A Mother's Resolve - Dante's POV

The penthouse felt different today, filled with a sense of anticipation that hummed through the air like electricity. I stood by the floor-to-ceiling windows, the sprawling view of New York City stretching out before me, but my thoughts were far from the skyline bathed in sunlight. My focus was on Alessia, who moved gracefully around the living room, her pregnancy becoming more pronounced with each passing week.

I watched her as she carefully arranged documents on the large oak table, a mixture of reports and strategies aimed at countering the threat from the Rivettis. The determination etched on her face made my heart swell with admiration. She was transforming before my eyes—blooming, not only into a mother but also into a fierce protector of our family.

"Dante?" Her voice drew me from my reverie, pulling me back to the present. I turned to see her looking at me with an intensity that demanded my attention. "I think we should consider expanding our reach to our allies. We need to ensure we have more support against Giovanni's maneuvers."

"Absolutely," I replied, stepping toward her. "This isn't just about you and me anymore; it's about our child and the legacy we want to build. We need to show strength and unity, especially now."

Alessia nodded, the fire in her eyes matching the resolve in my heart. I couldn't help but feel a profound sense of pride in how she was handling the challenges that loomed over us. The enemy was at our doorstep, and she was preparing to take an active role in safeguarding our family, ensuring our future was secure.

As she continued organizing the plans for our strategy, I allowed my gaze to linger on her. The way she carried herself had changed, imbued with a growing confidence that came from the knowledge of what lay ahead. I remembered the anxiety that shadowed her when she first learned of her pregnancy, the fear of the world we were bringing a child into.

But now, that fear was tempered with a fierce protective instinct that brought a relaxed strength I hadn't seen before.

"Do you want to lead the meeting with our allies?" I asked, gauging her readiness to take charge in such a significant way.

"Absolutely," she replied without hesitation. "I want them to see I'm as committed to our family's future as you are. They need to understand the stakes and why they should stand with us."

I felt a rush of warmth at her response. "You've become more than I ever imagined you would be, Alessia. Your strength astounds me, and I have no doubt that you'll impress our allies."

She smiled, her eyes sparkling with determination. "We're in this together. I want our child to grow up in a world where they feel safe, where they don't have to navigate the treachery that shadows our lives."

The very thought of our child grew my resolve. The desire to provide a nurturing world and a secure future for them pushed me forward. As it was, I had experienced too much darkness in my own life; I wouldn't allow it to consume my child. The notion of a child born into uncertainty was daunting but also thrilling, knowing we could break the cycle that had dominated our families for far too long.

"Let's finalize the details for our meeting with Gino and Marco," I proposed, directing her attention back to the table. "We have to ensure they understand our commitment to bolstering our defenses. If Luca is still in play, we cannot let our guard down."

Alessia was already moving through the papers, her fingers brushing over the various documents, nodding as she absorbed the information. "We need to outline exactly how Giovanni is attempting to exploit any perceived weaknesses in our operations. If we can expose his plans, we'll take the offensive before he can set his scheme into motion."

I stepped closer to her, our shared determination fueling the energy in the room. "You're right. If we can lock down our resources and rally our allies to our cause, it will send a powerful message to Giovanni and anyone foolish enough to follow him."

She paused, locking eyes with me, the weight of our shared responsibility clear as day. "I won't let anything happen to you, to us, or to our child," she stated, her voice resolute, confidence radiating from her. "We will not be defined by what others dictate—we are stronger than that."

In that moment, I couldn't deny the surge of pride welling within me. The world around us felt both menacing and vibrant, each heartbeat laced with the promise of a future worth fighting for. I reached out, tucking a strand of hair behind her ear, a small gesture of affection amidst the chaos. "We are stronger together."

The smile that broke across her face illuminated the room, a beacon of warmth amidst the cold realities we faced. But beneath the smile lay the steely determination that had come to define her. I knew that beneath her nurturing exterior lay a fierce warrior ready to face anything for the family we were building.

As the hours passed, we finalized our plans, our voices mingling with urgency as we laid out our next steps. Timing was critical, and every move we made needed to be calibrated to outmaneuver Giovanni. The challenges were mounting, but the fire in Alessia's heart ignited my own, reaffirming the path we were forging together.

"We should also consider reaching out to the Mancinis again," I suggested, recalling the fragile alliance we had formed. "Giovanni will be working relentlessly to undermine our hold, and we need their backing. We can set up a strategy session to remind them what's at stake."

"Agreed," Alessia said, thumbing through the documents to gather information regarding the Mancinis. "Their loyalty is still invaluable. If they see our commitment, they might amplify their support for us."

I could see her focus intensifying—this was a side of Alessia I had come to respect and admire. She was evolving into a partner not just in life but in battle, standing alongside me as we prepared to face our enemies head-on.

We spent the rest of the afternoon refining our strategies, alternating between tasks with an ease that came from deeply rooted trust. Every idea, suggestion, and piece of paper felt like a building block, constructing a fort of resistance against whatever storm awaited us.

As twilight set in, the city outside began to glow like a myriad of stars—a reminder of both the beauty and chaos intertwined within our lives. I felt a deep gratitude for these moments, for the glimmers of connection amidst a backdrop of uncertainty.

"Dante," Alessia said suddenly, breaking through my thoughts. "What about your family? Have you given any thought to how they impact our situation?"

The question hit me like a wave, and I felt the weight of my family's legacy settle heavy on my shoulders. "I've been thinking about it a lot lately. They embody a history of conflict, but I refuse to let that dictate our path. We are starting our own family, Alessia, and I want to create a legacy that is built on trust and loyalty."

Alessia smiled softly, her gaze piercing into me. "That's the legacy we need to build. One that ensures our child feels safe, loved, and supported. A future untainted by the past."

With each passing moment, I felt hope begin to blossom, intertwining with the resolve in my heart. Together, we would carve out a world distinct from the shadows that had haunted us for far too long.

"Nothing is more important than our family and our child," I said, feeling a swell of conviction. "You have my unwavering support, Alessia. You will lead us against Giovanni's advances, and I will be right there with you."

She stood still at my words, the soft lighting catching in her hair, making her look like something out of a dream. But she was no fantasy. She was real. She was mine.

"You trust me with this?" she asked, doubt in her eyes. "It is so important to get this meeting right…"

"I trust you with everything."

Her eyes shimmered, and in two steps she was in front of me. I reached for her, hands finding her waist, pulling her against me, the small swell of her stomach fitting perfectly between us.

"You're not just my fiancée, Alessia. You're the mother of my child. My partner. My equal. It's time they see you the way I do."

She leaned up and kissed me—soft at first, tentative. But I deepened it, needing her to feel every bit of what I meant. Her fingers slid into my hair, her body arching into mine like it always knew where to fit.

We moved together through the room, never breaking the kiss. I lifted her into my arms and carried her to the couch, laying her down with care. Reverence. Like she was both fire and miracle.

She looked up at me, eyes wide and full of emotion. "I love you," she whispered.

"Yes, baby," I murmured, brushing my thumb over her lips. "And I love you more than anything I've ever known."

I kissed her again, slower this time, my hands tracing the lines of her body with purpose. Every touch was a vow. Every breath a promise. This wasn't about lust—it was about connection, about claiming a future neither of us had dared to dream until now.

I moved with her, kissed down her throat, across her shoulder. She pulled me closer, her hands greedy for skin, and when we came together, it was with quiet gasps and whispered names. We moved in rhythm, our bodies speaking truths our hearts already knew.

After, I held her against my chest, her fingers trailing across my ribs.

"They'll follow you," I said into her hair. "Because I do."

She looked up at me, glowing with love and strength. "Together, we can break the cycle of fear and violence. We'll ensure our child grows up in a world where love reigns supreme."

And in that moment, with her in my arms and our child between us, I knew there was nothing we could not face.

Her words were like an anchor, steadying me amidst the uncertainty. In that moment, I understood that this was our fight—not just for survival, but for the future we had always envisioned. We would rise together, armed with strength and conviction, determined to shield our family from the encroaching darkness.

As we prepared for the road ahead, I knew one thing: Alessia was growing into the formidable mother I always knew she could be, a fierce warrior ready to protect our child. I would cherish that power in her, and together, we would withstand whatever challenges awaited.

Tonight, the penthouse was no longer just a living space; it felt like a sanctuary—a place where our family would thrive, a fortress against the world's threats. The love between us would serve as our greatest weapon, and together, we would embrace our new responsibilities, forging a brighter future in a world shadowed by uncertainty.

Chapter 15: A New Strategy - Alessia's POV

The room was dimly lit, the air thick with anticipation and tension as I stood at the head of the long, polished table. My heart beat steadily in my chest, each pulse a reminder of the magnitude of what lay ahead.

Tonight marked a crucial turning point—not just for our family but for the entire landscape of organized crime in New York City. The gathering of our potential allies at the Moretti estate felt like assembling a battalion for war, and I knew I had to be prepared to prove my worth as a leader.

The murmurs of conversation filled the room, an assortment of powerful mafia families whose allegiances could tip the balance against the Rivettis. Faces from various factions filled the chairs, each adorned with expressions ranging from skepticism to curiosity. This was no easy crowd; they were seasoned players in a game where the stakes were high and trust was a luxury few could afford.

I took a deep breath and stepped forward, keenly aware of the eyes upon me. "Thank you all for coming on such short notice. As you all know, we are here to discuss the growing threat posed by the Rivetti family and the need for united action against Giovanni's ambitions."

Vincenzo Mancini, seated at the far end of the table, nodded solemnly. "We're aware of the rumors surrounding Giovanni's latest moves and his attempts to undercut your businesses. This isn't just your problem; it's a threat to all of us in this city."

The murmurs of agreement echoed around the table, affirming the need for cooperation. I felt a surge of confidence; they were beginning to hear the urgency in my voice. "The Rivetti family is not just looking to expand their territory; they're attempting to monopolize the drug and gambling markets across the city. If we allow them to strengthen their position, it will destabilize everything we have built together."

"We need a strategy that not only counters Giovanni's threats but also strengthens our own operations," I continued, glancing around the table to gauge their reception. "By pooling our resources and sharing intelligence, we can keep the Rivetti family at bay while simultaneously expanding our influence."

"Go on," Marco urged, his supportive presence fueling my resolve as I spread the documents across the table, each visual aiding my plan.

"My proposal is simple but effective," I explained, gesturing to a chart detailing our existing routes and gambling hubs. "We can create a coalition that allows us to diversify and fortify our operations. By coordinating our drug supply lines, we can ensure that no single family is squeezed out of distribution. We can also establish joint ventures in gambling, combining our strengths to offer more enticing options to customers across the city."

A sense of intrigue settled in the room. I could see the minds of the different family heads whirring, contemplating how such an arrangement could benefit them. "We'll create loyalty programs that incentivize clients to engage with our coalition, ensuring they remain loyal to us and not the Rivettis. We'll offer promotions and packages people can't refuse."

"That sounds promising," Lorenzo D'Amato, a younger but ambitious leader among the families, chimed in. "But how can we ensure that our interests align and that no single family is left in the dust?"

"The key is transparency and fair distribution," I stated confidently. "We will lay out a detailed framework for sharing profits and resources, and all parties will have equal access to the information. In this way, no one family can leverage their position against the others. We're fighting a common enemy, and when we present a united front, we can overpower Giovanni's attempts to sow discord among us."

The room buzzed with a mix of skepticism and intrigue, but I could see alliances forming in the minds of my fellow leaders. This was a sensitive game we were playing, and I had to tread carefully. "I understand that trust needs to be built, and that it's not something given freely in this world. But imagine what we could accomplish together. If we can outmaneuver Giovanni by changing the game, we put ourselves in a position of strength."

"Strength in numbers has always been a difficult concept to grasp," remarked Vincenzo, his voice steady but lined with experience. "However, if we manage to convince our families to cooperate, it could indeed shift the dynamics in our favor."

"Exactly," I replied, leaning in to emphasize my point. "We turn the Rivettis into a side note in this city. Imagine the impact on their operations if we seize control of the main routes and leverage the gambling houses. We hold bigger cards, and we'll drive them out of the territories they currently threaten."

With each word I spoke, I felt a burgeoning sense of power blossoming within me. The prospect of building alliances, uniting our forces against Giovanni, increasingly excited me.

We possessed the ability to rewrite the narrative of our families' legacies.

"Let's talk about the drugs," Lorenzo interjected, his expression becoming more animated. "If we can create more supply lines that intersect, we can keep each other informed about fluctuations in our markets and eliminate any vulnerabilities. The Rivettis lose their hold, and we leverage partnerships to expand our reach."

"Yes, and we can also collaborate on logistics," I added, feeling encouraged by his enthusiasm. "Pooling our resources means we can handle transportation more efficiently, ensuring our products are delivered without interruption. If Giovanni gets wind of our plans, we'll have already disbanded his influence before he puts anything into motion."

The room erupted in muted discussions, families conferring with one another about the viability of executing such a strategy. I could feel the tide turning in our favor, a sense of unity beginning to emerge from the chaos.

Yet, I knew better than to believe it would be easy—The thoughts of previous betrayals loomed over us. "I must stress the importance of discretion during this process. Collusion and unforeseen fractures could allow Giovanni to exploit our weaknesses. We need to operate in the shadows, only revealing what's necessary to build trust."

Vincenzo spoke again, his voice firm. "I believe Alessia is right. We must establish protocols not only for sharing profits but also for guarding our activities from prying eyes. We can arrange a secure communication line to keep all parties informed discreetly."

With that, discussions unfolded around the table, bustling energy rippling in the air as potential allies started to see the vision. Conversations between factions sparked, creating excitement among those who had previously been hesitant. I felt a rush of hope as plans began to coalesce—united under a single strategy against Giovanni.

As the gathering progressed, a sense of unity began to crystallize, a common resolve growing within each family leader. The stakes were rising, shifting loyalties felt real, but for the first time in a long while, I could sense the possibility of change—a momentum that could reshape the very fabric of our dealings and upend the Rivetti stronghold.

"Together, we can reclaim our territories," I urged, a fire ignited within me, propelling me forward. "Let's strengthen our foundations and ensure our children inherit a world free from the suffocating greed that has plagued our families for too long. We'll show the Rivettis the true meaning of loyalty."

The families nodded, their acceptance and resolve taking shape in the dim lighting of the room. As I looked around, I knew this was just the beginning; the path ahead would require courage, but it was a path worth walking.

As we began drafting the final outline of our strategies, I felt a renewed sense of purpose coursing through me. There was no turning back now. This alliance could indeed shift the balance of power in our favor, but it would require every ounce of strength we collectively possessed.

With our plan solidified, I knew I had stepped into a role from which there was no retreat. I would fight tooth and nail for our family, our future, and the child I would soon bring into this world. As the discussions unfolded around me, I felt reinvigorated, ready to face whatever the Rivetti family would throw at us.

Tonight marked another turning point, and I was determined to ensure that we emerged victorious—stronger than we had ever been before.

Chapter 16: The Final Confrontation - Dante's POV

The abandoned warehouse loomed in the dying light of the evening, an ominous silhouette against the darkening sky. Once a bustling hub of activity, it now served as a ghostly backdrop for a confrontation I both dreaded and anticipated. The air was thick with tension, and I couldn't shake the feeling that we were walking straight into a storm. As I stood beside Alessia in the dimly lit interior, the creaking of the worn metal and the rustle of wind through broken windows echoed the unease thrumming in my chest.

Around us, the Moretti family, along with our newfound allies, moved quietly, preparing for the inevitable clash with the Rivetti family. We had spent hours strategizing, forming a united front to finally confront Giovanni and his men. The stakes were higher than ever—not just our positions within the city's criminal hierarchy, but the very safety of Alessia and our unborn child.

"Dante," Alessia interrupted my thoughts, her voice steady but laced with urgency as she placed a hand on her belly. "Are you sure we're ready for this?"

I turned to her, my heart swelling at the sight of her fierce determination despite the weight of impending motherhood. "We've prepared for this, Alessia. We'll handle whatever comes our way. You just focus on staying calm."

Her eyes shone with unwavering resolve, yet I could see the strain of her pregnancy start to take its toll. "Promise me you'll protect us," she said, squeezing my hand tightly.

"Always," I promised, my grip firm. "You and the baby are my priority."

I didn't think there would be violence tonight. Tonight, we talk. We lay out our expectations and we hear theirs. Then, if we can't come back with an agreement, I might expect some escalation.

As we shared a fleeting moment of connection, the room exploded with the sounds of voices rising in a chorus of anxious murmurs. The other families were assembling; bonds were being forged anew, and every leader was steeling themselves for the battle that lay ahead. When we had first formed this alliance, I could never have anticipated the storm we now faced.

Just as I was about to organize our final details, the heavy steel door creaked open, breaking the tense silence. Figures began to shuffle in, and I squared my shoulders as I recognized Giovanni's men, faces hidden beneath masks and attitudes steeped in violence. Tension rippled through our ranks.

"Get ready," I whispered, my senses sharpening as adrenaline coursed through my veins. "They're here."

A flicker of movement caught my eye just as the familiar sound of chuckling echoed through the warehouse. I caught sight of Giovanni himself, flanked by several of his most loyal enforcers, their eyes gleaming with malevolent confidence. He stepped into the flickering light, a smug smile curling his lips as he surveyed the scene.

"Dante!" he called out, his voice dripping with disdain. "I thought you'd put up more of a fight! Look at this pathetic little gathering."

"Speak for yourself, Giovanni," I shot back, stepping forward, my fists clenched. "This isn't over, and you know it."

Giovanni's laughter echoed through the cavernous space, sending shivers down my spine. "Oh, but it is. You see, I've grown tired of your petty attempts to challenge my authority. And tonight, I plan on ending this once and for all."

Without warning, his men surged forward, a swell of bodies driven by firepower and unyielding loyalty. I was shocked by their audacity. This isn't the way things were done.

Bullets ripped through the air, and the world around us exploded into chaos. I felt the deafening crack of gunfire, the smell of gunpowder and adrenaline mingling in the air, as I instinctively pulled Alessia behind me, shielding her from the onslaught.

"Stay down!" I shouted, pushing her to the floor as a hail of bullets shattered glass and ricocheted off the metallic structures around us. The once quiet warehouse became a theater of violence, chaos spiraling out of control as I shifted my focus to the battle at hand.

Gunshots reverberated with terrifying intensity, echoing off the steel walls, making it nearly impossible to decipher where each shot came from. The Moretti family responded with fierce determination, taking their positions, returning fire, providing cover for one another as we fought back against Giovanni's relentless assault.

"Dante!" I heard Marco shout amidst the chaos as he moved skillfully around the perimeter, bullets whizzing past him. "We need to regroup! We can't let them pin us down here!"

"Let's push forward!" I yelled back, adrenaline fueling my every move. The stakes had never been higher, and the unpredictable nature of battle only sharpened my instincts. I had to protect Alessia, our child, and our family—whatever it took.

Rushing forward, I took cover behind a decrepit crate as my pulse quickened. The sharp sound of gunfire and the grunts of my allies filled the air, mingling with the metallic scent of blood and the dread of battle. I caught a glimpse of Giovanni's men pressing in from all sides, their confidence juxtaposed with our brandished weapons, and I could feel the tide shifting, our fate intertwined with each act of defiance.

Before I could rally my thoughts, the echoing sound of Alessia gasping broke through the chaos, pulling my attention toward her. I turned just in time to see her clutching her belly, her face growing pale as a wave of panic washed over her.

"Alessia! What's wrong?" I demanded, fear gripping me like a vice.

"I… I think it's starting," she gasped, her breath coming out in sharp bursts, panic lacing her words. "The contractions… they're happening!"

The icy grip of terror seized my heart. "No, not now!" I howled, fighting against the impossibility of our situation. We were in the middle of a war zone, and the thought of her going into labor amid all this madness sent chills spiraling through me.

"Dante, I can't—" she cried, her voice trembling as another contraction hit, making her gasp in pain. I rushed to her side, wracking my mind for a solution, then looked into her eyes, which reflected both fear and resilience.

"We have to get out of here," I urged, my heart racing. "I can't let you face this here! I'll get you to safety."

"No, I can't go," she insisted, gripping my arm tightly. "We have to help our family. They need us."

I understood the fierce loyalty that fueled her, the unwavering strength that defined her character—but the reality of the situation forced me to flood with protective instincts. "You're more important than any of this, Alessia! If anything happens to you or the baby, I won't forgive myself."

"I won't abandon our family to this!"

Before I could argue further, the chaos erupted anew—the dull thud of an explosion rang out, shaking the ground as debris fell from above. I instinctively pushed Alessia deeper into our cover, trying to shield her from the danger surrounding us.

The sound of shouted orders rang throughout the space as I regrouped with my allies, my eyes scanning for leads in this desperate battle. "We need to push them back!" I bellowed at Marco and Gino beside me. "We can't allow them to overwhelm us!"

The fire from our weapons raged on, but the Rivettis fought with relentless fervor, driven by Giovanni's ambition as they pushed against our barricades. That same ambition felt like a tidal wave crashing against our defenses, and I knew the intensity of our fight would escalate the longer we remained trapped here.

In the back of my mind, I felt the danger of Alessia's contractions—each one a symbol of both fragility and resilience. She was fighting to bring new life into this world even amid chaos. Just then, I caught a glimpse of Giovanni, seething with rage as he barked orders to his men.

"Focus your fire on them!" Giovanni shouted, his arrogance proving to be his greatest flaw. "Don't let them escape!"

A sudden surge of determination ignited in me. "No more running," I muttered under my breath, the protective instinct for my family overriding everything else. "We end this here."

"I'm with you," Marco affirmed, his eyes burning with resolve. "Let's fight fire with fire."

We surged forward, pushing against the tide of Rivetti enforcers, forcing our way through relentless gunfire while providing cover for one another. A new adrenaline rush surged through me with each thunderous gunshot; the fight was palpable, every heartbeat fueling the urgency of our cause.

"Dante!" Alessia's voice cut through the chaos once more. My heart twisted as I saw her struggling to remain calm, the strain of impending labor evident in her wrinkled brow.

"I need you to be strong for me; I'll be right back," I said, a sudden determination igniting within me as I kissed her forehead, a brief moment of clarity amidst the storm. "Hold on."

As I plunged back into the chaos, the sounds of gunfire and shouts enveloped me, but I was steadfast as I fought through the fray. I needed to reach Giovanni, to confront him head-on, to dismantle his ambition.

As I cornered an advancing group of Rivetti enforcers, I made my move, launching myself at them. The adrenaline coursed through my veins like wildfire, and I felt the power surge through me as fists met flesh, bodies hit the ground, and gunfire thundered above. In that moment, everything faded except the driving force pushing me to protect my family.

Just as I closed in on Giovanni, I heard the sound of a scream—a visceral cry that cut through the clamor of gunfire. My heart raced—Alessia. I turned toward her, panic gripping my chest.

"Alessia!" I shouted, but another gunshot rang out nearby, the explosion of chaos pushing me back. I fought through a haze, overwhelming despair threatening to consume me as I continued to fight my way through the fray.

Reaching the edge of the central conflict, I was finally able to see across the battlefield, and there she was: Alessia sitting against the wall, her face contorted in pain as she grabbed hold of her belly. With a steely resolve, she began to push through the contractions, determination radiating from her.

In that moment, I felt everything else drain away. My mission to confront Giovanni was eclipsed by the need to return to her side. "Stay with me, Alessia!" I yelled, but chaos ensued as shields collapsed, and the Rivetti men began to overpower our lines.

The battle raged on, but I could feel a new focus sharpening within me. I charged back toward her, knowing I couldn't let anything happen to my family. I weaved through the chaos, matching my fury to my need for her safety.

"Dante!" Alessia cried one last time, her voice a mix of agony and resolve as I moved to her side, her fingers tightly gripping my own. "Alessia, I'm here!" I desperately reassured her, crouching down and taking her hand firmly. "I've got you. We're going to get through this together."

"Make them stop fighting! I can't do this while they're around!" she pleaded, her voice teetering on desperation. The urgency in her tone lit a fire within me.

"We'll end this," I vowed, my eyes locking onto the chaotic melee before us. I could feel the weight of the world pressing down on me, the noise fading as the reality of parenthood collided with the brutality around us. "You're not alone."

Beyond us, gunfire flared again as the Rivettis pushed forward, willing to risk everything to maintain their empire. But I would not allow them to take away my family. I glared at Giovanni, who was still roaring commands over the chaos, and I felt my heart burn with anger.

In that moment, I resolved myself to one singular truth: no amount of ambition or greed could take away my love for

Alessia and our child. "You will not take her away from me," I promised, the weight of my vow igniting my very soul.

As screams echoed around us, I took a deep breath and prepared to launch forward once more into the fray, ready to face down Giovanni. The battle around us would not define our fate; it would be our love and determination that would bring forth the light of a new beginning.

Tonight would not end in chaos. It wouldn't mark our defeat. Today, we would rise above the darkness—and I was determined to ensure my family emerged unscathed no matter the cost.

Chapter 17: Sacrifices Made - Alessia's POV

The air was thick with smoke and the acrid scent of gunpowder as I sat against the cold, unforgiving wall of the warehouse. I could barely hear the chaos around me, the sounds of shouting and gunfire fading into a haunting echo. My heart raced, but not solely from the adrenaline of battle; it was the overwhelming reality of the moments that had just transpired. I cradled my belly, feeling the life within me stir, and I couldn't shake the fear that gripped my heart.

Dante had promised he would protect me, and now I clung to that promise as I processed the moments leading up to this. The confrontation with the Rivettis had spiraled into violence faster than I could have imagined. I had witnessed courage, chaos, and sacrifice—each more profound than the last.

"Alessia!" Dante's voice broke through the haze, drawing me from my thoughts. I looked up to see him rushing toward me, wild-eyed and determined, but his expression shifted the moment he caught sight of me. "Are you okay?"

"I'm fine," I lied, forcing a smile even as another wave of pain surged through me. "But... what happened?"

His face was lined with exhaustion and fear. "We lost men—good men. The Rivettis fought harder than we anticipated. But we held our ground; Giovanni's forces were pushed back," he said, glancing over his shoulder toward the ongoing chaos. "Now we just need to regroup and tend to everyone. We have to make sure they're safe."

I felt a heavy weight settle upon my chest as the implications of his words registered. Good men lost. Sacrifices made. I looked around the dimly lit warehouse, noting fallen figures draped across the floor—those we had called allies. The harsh reality cut deep, a bitter reminder that the world we inhabited demanded blood and loyalty at every turn.

"I can't believe this is what it's come to," I said, my voice trembling. "All of it—this violence, these choices that rip families apart. I wanted to protect our child, to build a better future, not turn to this..."

"The reality of our lives is brutal, Alessia." Dante knelt beside me, his eyes fierce and filled with an intensity I admired. "We take risks—every day, every choice we make—and sometimes, sacrifices are necessary. But know this: it wasn't in vain. We stood united, and we pushed back against the Rivettis. Our child will be born into a world where we will fight for their future."

I pressed my eyes shut, fighting the tears that threatened to spill over. "But at what cost, Dante? We may have won this battle, but we lost so much. Families torn apart and lives lost. How can we ever recover from this?"

He took my hands in his, grounding me in a moment where the chaos felt far away. "As long as we have each other, we will recover. We'll lean on our family, our allies, and we will ensure that those sacrifices made tonight will not define who we are. We have to hold onto that—especially for our child."

The reality of my choices gnawed at me, leaving a trail of uncertainty. I looked away, scanning the remnants of the chaos—the lifeless bodies, the echoes of cries, and the shattered dreams that had been unraveled in the name of survival. My heart burned, torn between the love I felt for my family and the sorrow that now enveloped me.

I felt the contractions ease up, heard Dante bark out orders for someone to get us a car and alert the private hospital that we were on our way in—that tonight, our baby could be born.

"Those not fallen here today will remember the sacrifice," I murmured. "But how can I make peace with it? How can I accept that we had to go this far?"

Dante shifted closer, his voice steady yet filled with vulnerability. "You don't need to accept it all at once. This life comes with its complexities, Alessia. But we have to keep moving forward. We owe it to those who stood by us—those who fell while defending our family. We can honor their memories by ensuring their sacrifice was not in vain."

I searched his eyes, and in that moment, I understood the weight he bore. The anguish behind his gaze matched my own—a shared burden that engrossed both of us. The stakes had never felt higher, and the world we sought to protect felt crueler than ever.

Before I could respond, an anguished cry echoed through the warehouse, jolting me back to the present. I turned, my heart racing at the sight of Marco kneeling beside a fallen figure—one of our allies. Blood mixed with dust on the floor, cementing the gravity of our reality.

"No! No!" Marco yelled, desperation and pain flooding his voice. I watched helplessly as he cradled the lifeless body of a friend, his anguish raw and palpable. It was a sight that cut deeper than any wound I could imagine; the loss he faced reminded me of how fleeting life could be and the weight of the sacrifices we must carry.

I felt Dante's presence beside me as he steeled himself, intentionally hardening his expression at the pain unfolding. "Marco," he called. "We need to focus. We can't let this distract us from regrouping and making sure everyone is safe."

The sorrowful expression on Marco's face was striking. "How can you say that?" he shouted, his voice rising in anguish. "We just lost him! He was part of our family! Who will pay for this? What's the point if we're losing our own?"

His words struck chords of fear in me, a resonance between grief and anger that felt all too real. I turned back toward Dante, but the grim look on his face told me he understood how fragile our convictions had become.

"Listen, Marco," he said firmly, yet with compassion. "We owe it to him and everyone else to continue fighting. They believed in us. They sacrificed everything to protect what we have. If we let despair consume us, then it has all been for nothing."

The conviction of his words seemed to hang in the air like an unbreakable bond. Slowly, Marco's anger began to dissipate, replaced by the painful reality of necessity—the truth that had brought so many of us here.

I felt that bond as well, the energy between our family, igniting an unyielding resolve within me. Yes, sacrifices had been made—too many sacrifices. But in the face of unfathomable loss, we had to rally together as a family.

"Let's honor their memory by showing that we can rise above this violence," I urged, my voice steady with emotion. "Let's stand together and ensure their sacrifices weren't in vain. We owe it to them to keep our family intact, to provide a better future for our children."

With those words, I could see a shift across the faces in the room. There was an understanding among us now, a rallying cry echoing through the grief. Pain and sacrifice would become part of our stories, but they wouldn't define us. Instead, they would become the fuel for fighting back and reclaiming what was rightfully ours.

As we began to pick ourselves up, I felt a surge of determination blending with the mounting sorrow. Each choice brought with it a weight—one we would bear together. We may have suffered losses, but tonight would become a stepping stone into a future we could shape together.

The warehouse that had once been a backdrop for chaos now felt like a sacred ground, a place infused with the memories of those we had lost. It was a reminder that we were still here, still standing—fighting for our family and for a future I believed we could create.

With Dante's hand resting firmly in mine, I stood stronger than before, resolute in my commitment to protect our child and ensure our family's legacy thrived. We had been tested, but together we would rise up against the shadows, shaping a new path forged from love and resilience.

As the dust began to settle, I gathered my strength and the resolve to navigate the unknown ahead. The sacrifices made became not only a memory but a catalyst for choice—the choice to carry forward, to fight fiercely, and to protect the family that meant everything to me. Our future awaited, and I would be ready to embrace it.

Chapter 18: Healing Wounds - Dante's POV

The penthouse felt different in the aftermath of the confrontation, a palpable shift settling over our lives. The remnants of chaos had begun to fade, replaced by an atmosphere charged with the potential for healing and renewal. I sat on the expansive terrace overlooking the pulsing heart of New York City, the skyline a muted backdrop against the rising sun. The shadows of the past still lingered, but in their wake, a sense of hope began to blossom.

As I sipped my coffee, I watched Alessia move through the large living space, a gentle yet powerful presence that filled the room. She was tending to our newborn, cradling our child with a tenderness that stole my breath. Seeing her this way, radiant and nurturing, made me feel both awed and humbled. The battle we fought had tested us in unfathomable ways, but witnessing the strength she embodied fueled my determination to rebuild our family and our legacy.

After the brutal confrontation with Giovanni and the Rivetti family, we faced a double-edged sword: the wounds of loss and grief were still fresh, yet the spirit of resilience encouraged us to forge ahead. We would not be defined by the chaos of our lives; we would rise again.

"Dante," Alessia called softly, breaking my reverie. I turned to see her approach, a gentle smile spreading across her face despite the weariness in her eyes. "It's a beautiful morning, isn't it?"

"It is," I replied, setting down my cup and moving to her side. "The calm after the storm feels promising."

Alessia nodded, glancing toward the horizon where the sun bathed the city in warm light. "It feels like a new beginning."

It certainly was. The alliance we had forged with other mafia families was beginning to show its fruits, and I couldn't help but feel a swell of pride. What had started as a desperate measure for survival transformed into a coalition that promised greater strength and stability for our families and the streets of New York.

"We need to summon everyone soon," I said, still gazing across the city. "It's time to affirm our commitments and solidify the advantages of our new alliances."

I watched as Alessia turned thoughtful. "It's crucial that we present a strong front, especially after everything that's happened. The last thing we need is for anyone to see us as weak."

"Exactly," I confirmed, my mind buzzing with our plans. The fallout from the Rivetti confrontation had forced us to rethink our position. The Mancinis, D'Amatos, and even the Costas had been eager to join forces, recognizing the value of solidarity in a ruthless landscape where loyalty was often bought and sold.

"We will call upon them," I continued. "After what we've endured, we need to show our strength—not just for us, but for the families who understand the stakes involved. They need to know we will stand by each other in this fight."

Alessia placed a hand on my arm, her touch grounding me as she met my gaze. "I believe in this, Dante. Together, we can safeguard our futures—our child's future. This is about more than just us; it's about our families and the legacy we leave behind."

Her words resonated within me. This was a pivotal moment, an opportunity to transcend the violence and chaos that had once defined our lives. If love could spur us into action, then perhaps we could create a world free from the shadows that had threatened to consume us.

***

Later that afternoon, the atmosphere of the penthouse shifted once more as our allies began to arrive. The spacious living room, normally elegant and subtle, swelled with the presence of powerful figures from across the realm of organized crime. Each family brought their own history, their loyalties hanging in the air like a taut wire.

I stood at the center of the room, feeling the weight of their gazes upon me as I prepared to speak. To my left, Vincenzo Mancini stood tall and proud, embodying the confidence that came from years of experience in our world. He had been a vital ally throughout the recent conflict and had rallied his family to our cause with an unwavering loyalty that forged a bond between us.

To my right, Lorenzo D'Amato listened intently, his eyes shining with determination—the kind of fiery spirit essential in our line of work. He had shown himself to be just as fierce and devoted to this family as any older man, and his partnership with us was an unshakeable force within the coalition.

Elena stood near Marco. I bit back a rueful smile. Those two had been secretly in love for years. I wondered when they would finally do something about it.

Luca lounged against a wall, arms crossed, eyeing the assembly. He had been eager to join us after the confrontation, to prove himself once again. He was young, impressionable. He would learn soon enough how important it was to pick sides. His natural charisma lent itself well to building relationships with those around him. His family were crucial to have on our side, able to leverage their influence as they controlled several lucrative gambling establishments throughout the city.

Antonio was not here today. Though he was firmly on our side again, trust had been broken. It would take years before it was rebuilt.

"The loyalty we forge here today is vital to our mutual survival," I began, capturing the attention of those gathered. "The Rivettis may have tried to sow discord, but we will not be intimidated. We are stronger together, united under the common goal of protecting our families and the territories we've built with our sweat and blood."

A ripple of agreement flowed through the room, heads nodding as I scanned their faces. The collective weight of their shared histories reminded me of the stakes at hand, a reality we could no longer ignore.

"The numbers alone can shift the balance of power," I continued. "But we also recognize the value of trust. We must be transparent about our operations, and each clan should share intelligence without fear of reprisal. To ensure our territories thrive, we have to watch each other's backs."

As I spoke, I felt the energy swell around me. The alliances formed were one of mutual benefit, combining resources and networks to create a web of influence stronger than any one family could muster alone.

"It's not just about preserving what we have, but expanding what we can achieve as a coalition," Vincenzo added, standing beside me, his presence commanding respect. "With our combined footholds in the drug trade and gambling sectors, we can push back hard against Giovanni's ambitions. We seize control of routes, tighten supply lines, and present a united front that cannot be broken."

The room erupted into a chorus of agreement, voices rising as leaders exchanged strategies and ideas, excitement bubbling over among the assembled families. It was exhilarating to see them engage, each in their element, understanding the stakes that their families faced.

I watched as Alessia interacted with those present, engaging in rhetoric that reminded me of our shared dreams. She was no longer just the mother of my child; she was becoming a key player, embodying the fierce spirit of this moment. It filled me with pride to see her stepping into her strength, not only for herself but for our family's future.

Marco made his way through the room, his presence sturdy as he added valuable insight, ensuring that every voice was heard and every opinion counted. He had been a vital ally throughout this ordeal, and the bond that formed from adversity had only made us stronger.

As discussions flowed, I felt a renewed sense of purpose. The alliances we were forging went beyond individual gains; they represented a mutual commitment to protect our families, to create a legacy free from the fears we had endured for too long.

"We can take back our neighborhoods!" Luca declared passionately, the fervor in his voice igniting the energy in the room. "Let's establish territories that are not only profitable but safe for our families. We drive out threats like the Rivettis and ensure no one dares challenge our authority again."

The determination in the air was infectious, and I could feel the room rallying together, a newfound strength replacing previous doubts and fears.

With every new alliance formed, with every bond strengthened amid shared struggles, I felt the weight of my past lift slightly. Here, together, we were crafting a future that sought to break the cycle of violence and fear—a future where our children could thrive, unshackled by the burdens that had bound us.

As the meeting began to wind down, I felt a wave of gratitude wash over me. The families who had gathered had shown that we could overcome adversity by standing unified—a lesson that resonated deeper than any agreement or alliance.

Together, we were creating a sanctuary against the chaos that threatened to consume the world around us. We had turned from fractured groups into a formidable coalition, ready to face whatever challenges loomed on the horizon. The dawn had arrived, a bright promise illuminated against yesterday's shadows.

In the days to come, the work would be arduous, but I was resolute. As I looked around at the faces of our allies and the burgeoning strength of our coalition, I felt it: we had all made sacrifices, but those sacrifices would not be for nothing. We would forge ahead into the unknown, carving a path that honored the fallen and celebrated the bonds that united us.

The Moretti family would not only survive—we would thrive, stronger and more resolute than ever before. With

Alessia and our newborn at my side, I could face whatever the future might hold. Together, we would reclaim our world, one step at a time.

Chapter 19: A Family United - Alessia's POV

The air was filled with a sense of joy and celebration as light cascaded through the grand windows of the Moretti family estate. The room was adorned with vibrant flowers and decorations that seemed to dance in tune with the laughter of our gathered friends and family. It felt unreal, a beautiful dream woven together with warmth and love.

In the center of it all was a sense of transcendence—a moment of pure happiness that had arrived after the chaos and turmoil we had endured. I cradled our newborn baby in my arms, the weight of this miraculous life suddenly eclipsing all the hardships. The soft coos and little breaths from my child filled the air with a new kind of hope that I hadn't fully comprehended until now; it was a hope that made the sacrifices we had all made feel worthwhile.

As I looked around the room, the laughter and camaraderie among the assembled mafia families brought a swell of pride to my heart. Today was not only a celebration of my child's birth but a testament to the bonds we had forged through our trials.

"Alessia!" I heard Vincenzo Mancini's voice cut through the joyful chaos, and I turned to see him striding towards me, a broad smile on his face. "I have a gift for your little one."

"Thank you, Vincenzo," I replied, my heart swelling as he presented a beautifully crafted silver rattle. It gleamed like a star in the sunlight, an heirloom that would carry the weight of history within our families. "It's beautiful."

He nodded, looking pleased. "May it bring your child the same strength that has characterized our families for generations. This little one represents a future we can shape together."

As I watched him move through the crowd, greeting guests with a warmth that belied his formidable exterior, I couldn't help but feel that the alliances we'd formed had become more than just business. They were rooted in a newfound trust, a commitment to raise our children in a world that promised safety and stability amid the chaos of our lives.

Maria Moretti approached next, a radiant smile lighting up her face as she presented a lovely hand-knitted blanket. "For the sweet little one," she said, her voice filled with genuine affection. "I hope it provides warmth and comfort in the years to come."

"Thank you, Maria. It's beautiful," I replied, receiving the blanket with care. It felt personal, a token of love that represented the strong familial bonds we were building.

With every passing moment, guests continued to arrive, heads of mafia families bringing gifts that spoke of the respect they held for the Moretti family. Luca entered, a glint of mischief in his eyes as he bore a small, expertly crafted wooden horse—a symbol of protection for our child.

"Every child deserves a guardian to watch over them," he said, handing it over with a grin. "Just in case their parents ever get too distracted with all the chaos."

I chuckled softly at his charm, grateful for the lightness he brought amidst the weightiness of our lives. "Thank you, Luca. I'll make sure to keep it close."

As the celebration continued, I felt a wave of joy sweeping over me, grounding me in the moment. The laughter of children mingled with the excitement of adults sharing stories, new alliances tying us together in this joyous occasion. Family ties were being cemented, brick by brick, through this shared experience.

"Isn't it incredible?" Elena said as she approached, her eyes sparkling. "All these powerful families coming together, not just to celebrate but to affirm your strength as a leader. It's beautiful to see how they respect you."

I glanced at Marco, never far from Elena these days, then back at Elena. "Am I right in assuming your life might soon take a… romantic turn?"

She smiled wistfully. "I'm still figuring that out. I want to make my own path for myself. You know, a career. Something that is mine."

I smiled back at her, a warmth blossoming in my chest. "I have a feeling that you will figure it all out soon enough." I looked around us. "It feels surreal. The love and support surrounding my baby somehow amplifies the joy of the moment. Each gift is more than just an item—it's a symbol of trust and commitment moving forward."

Suddenly, the doors swung open, and in walked Dante, a welcoming smile lighting up his face as he approached. "Alessia! You look radiant!" His gaze fell to the small bundle in my arms. "And I see our little one is already the center of attention."

I felt my heart flutter at the sight of him, his presence a grounding force in the whirlwind of celebration. "Just a small gathering—nothing too grand," I replied teasingly.

"Nothing too grand?" he chuckled, shaking his head. "This is phenomenal! Our families are united, and they're celebrating the new beginning of our legacy."

The room buzzed with energy, the atmosphere electric with the promise of alliances solidified in the face of adversity. The laughter and chatter radiated warmth, echoing with every heartbeat of our gathering. My heart swelled as I watched the heads of families come together, unified by this moment.

"Have you seen the arrangements?" Dante asked, referring to the endless stream of gifts and tokens gathered around the room. "They're showing their respect—and forging trust."

I nodded, feeling a rush of gratitude. "It's astonishing to see how far we've come—not just as individuals, but as families. This little one holds the key to a future we can reshape together."

As we moved through the gathering, I could feel the love and support from everyone around us. Technically, we had united under shared hardships, and now we were forging solid connections built on loyalty and respect. Each new alliance reaffirmed our commitment to protecting one another, ensuring that the dangers of our reality would not overshadow our children's lives.

Later, as I settled into a comfortable space, I felt the warmth of my newborn nestled against my chest. The small, rhythmic breathing felt like a heartbeat of hope, a symbol that we could create something beautiful even amidst chaos and uncertainty. This little life blossomed out of the joys and pains of our world, representing the night's ambitions.

Dante sat beside me, taking my hand in his as we both watched the crowd celebrating around us. "I can't help but feel that tonight truly marks a new chapter for us," he said quietly, his voice full of promise.

"It does," I replied, leaning into him. "We're forging bonds that matter—that transcend past grievances and build toward futures that let our children grow up in a world where they won't have to fight every day just to belong."

His eyes sparkled with hope, a reflection of the strength that surging through us both. "We will work together to protect and nurture this life we've brought into the world. Through the darkness, we will carve out a future illuminated by love."

As the celebration unfolded, I felt a sense of serenity. The laughter and music enveloped us, nurturing our spirits and solidifying the connection among our families. Bonds forged in adversity are often the strongest, and I was confident that we would rise to any challenge that lay ahead.

In that moment, cradling our child against my heart, I understood with every fiber of my being that we would weather whatever storms would come. Together as a united family, we would redefine our legacy, living boldly in love and loyalty as we embraced the beautiful chaos of our lives.

As the evening drew on, filled with joy and celebration, I felt the comfort of togetherness weave through our gathering. All the families were here, committed to protecting what mattered most—the future of our children and the unity we now cherished. This was just the beginning, a foundation upon which we would build a world unlike anything we had known before.

And as I gazed at the little one resting in my arms, I realized that our journey was far from over; it was only just beginning.

Chapter 20: New Beginnings - Dante's POV

The streets of New York buzzed with an energy that felt electric, a cacophony of sounds and sights that pulsed through the city as I walked alongside Alessia. It was a vibrant tapestry of life—taxi horns blaring, vendors shouting, and the hum of conversations weaving in and out of the various storefronts lining the streets. The air was thick with potential, and with each step, I could feel the weight of new beginnings pressing against us.

Alessia had stepped into her role with an unwavering confidence, transforming from a supportive partner into a powerful figure in her own right within the family. The transformation had sparked something within her—a determination to redefine not only her identity but the very legacy of the Moretti family. Watching her move through the crowds, poised and radiant, I couldn't help but swell with pride. She was ready to carve her own path in a world that had once seemed so daunting.

Over the past weeks, as she embraced her new role, I witnessed her strengths flourish before my eyes. The past year had weighed heavily on her shoulders, but now, a renewed sense of purpose seemed to radiate from her. She was no longer content to stand in the shadows; she wanted to lead and to ensure that our child would grow up in a world where love and loyalty prevailed over chaos and violence.

"Dante," Alessia said, breaking the spell of my thoughts as she gingerly tucked a strand of hair behind her ear. "We need to head to the East Side later. I've set up meetings with some potential partners."

Her enthusiasm sparked a fire within me. "You're really diving in headfirst, aren't you?" I teased, grinning at her determination.

"Absolutely," she replied, her eyes gleaming with excitement. "It's time for the Morettis to expand our influence. We've laid the groundwork with our allies, but now it's time to solidify our standing in the market—a move that will redefine our family's legacy for generations to come."

"I'm all for it," I affirmed, feeling a surge of excitement at the thought of the plans she had brewing. "What do you have in mind?"

Alessia shot me a playful glance, clearly relishing her newfound authority. "We're going to expand our operations beyond the usual territories. I want to invest in legitimate businesses to integrate our influence into the community. By connecting with local entrepreneurs and offering support, we can create partnerships that benefit everyone involved. It's time to rebuild trust between our families and the community."

The more she spoke, the clearer her vision became. I could see it in her posture, the way she carried herself—as if she were ready to take on the world. "You're right," I replied, nodding thoughtfully. "By fostering legitimate businesses, we can create a façade of respectability that solidifies our position while providing a safe environment for our family and allies."

"Yes," she replied enthusiastically. "We can shape a new narrative—one that isn't steeped in the violence that has haunted our families for so long. People need to see that we are committed to the community, helping residents thrive, all while maintaining our operations beneath the surface."

The possibilities unfolded before me, the vision she painted igniting a spark within me. "You'll create a legacy that instills pride in our family name, Alessia. This is the beginning of something incredible."

We continued walking through the bustling streets, eclectic energy swirling around us, infused with the laughter and chatter of people living their lives. I watched her take in the scene, noting her growing excitement as she mentally scouted potential locations and opportunities.

"We can open a community center," she said, a new idea spilling forth. "Somewhere that provides job training and support for business development—giving people skills they can use while also creating connections with us. It'll strengthen our influence and build loyalty, rooted in goodwill rather than fear."

The air buzzed around us with the rhythm of her ideas taking shape. "And we can integrate our actual businesses into the community. Made-in-New-York artisanal products, perhaps?" she continued. "That puts us on people's radar for the right reasons."

"I like where this is headed," I replied, feeling the adrenaline surge through me. "Not only will we shape a better future for our child, but we will also build a network that supports the families in the neighborhoods we operate in. It's a powerful way to redefine our identity as a family."

As we strolled past the storefronts, I could envision what this would look like—an ever-expanding network of support, transforming the lives of those around us while simultaneously establishing our presence as benevolent leaders instead of feared adversaries.

We soon found ourselves at a small café with a vibrant atmosphere, bustling patrons enjoying their afternoon break. Alessia turned to me, her eyes sparkling as she gestured to the bustling scene. "This could be a great first partnership. I'll be meeting with the owner soon to discuss how we might collaborate to expand their reach—help introduce local artistry and products through delivery services."

"I love it," I said, imagining the scene as she spoke. "The partnerships will drive traffic into their business while we establish goodwill in the community. We'll support their growth, and in return, they'll help us integrate smoothly into the fabric of the neighborhoods."

In that moment, I couldn't help but marvel at her vision. She had taken the trials we faced and transformed them into an opportunity—a chance to reclaim our family's narrative and base it in strength and unity.

"Let's go inside," she suggested, her eyes glimmering with excitement. "We can familiarize ourselves with the space, and you can meet the owner. I want you to see her passion for her craft."

As we entered the café, a soft bell chimed overhead, and the warm scent of freshly brewed coffee filled the air. We were greeted by the upbeat energy that buoyed the atmosphere, and within moments, Alessia had struck up a conversation with the barista before turning to me with a spark of joy.

"This is what I envision, Dante," she said, her voice filled with enthusiasm reverberating through the room. "A place that not only focuses on serving the community but also encourages dialogue among families. We can help cultivate a sense of belonging, trust, and collaboration amongst all involved."

I took a moment to soak it all in—the bright smiles of patrons and the vibrant chatter that filled the air. It was a striking representation of community coming together, a perfect epitome of what Alessia hoped to achieve. The possibilities for growth felt boundless.

As we sipped our drinks, I felt the intensity of the moment wash over me. "With your commitment and vision, the Morettis will step out of the shadows and into the light," I said. "Our child will grow up in a world where our family's legacy is one of empowerment rather than fear. We'll leave behind a legacy that symbolizes the strength of community, innovation, and trust."

"We have the chance to be something greater," Alessia replied, a fire dancing in her eyes. "To reshape our identities, show the world that we're capable of more than what they might perceive us to be." Her enthusiasm reverberated through me like a ripple in water, a burgeoning hope blooming in the depths of my heart.

With Alessia at the helm, ready to tackle the world head-on, I could feel the weight of the past receding, making way for the bright horizon ahead. The sunlight streaming through the café windows seemed to illuminate our path, guiding us toward a future steeped in promise.

"I'm behind you every step of the way, Alessia," I vowed, leaning closer to her. "You're formidable, and together, there's nothing we can't accomplish."

As she smiled back at me, her determination radiated into the world, a beacon of light encouraging progress and growth. Our story was evolving—filled with hope and resilience—and I could not be more proud to stand by her side as we forged new beginnings together.

In the bustling heart of New York, between the noise of everyday life and the promise of tomorrow, we were building a future where our legacy would thrive—not just for our family, but for the city we called home.

Chapter 20: Legacy of Power - Dante's POV

The Moretti estate stood tall against the backdrop of the New York skyline, a beacon of resilience and strength that encapsulated everything we had fought for. The sprawling grounds were meticulously groomed, lush green gardens stretching out like a sanctuary amidst the chaos of the city, reflecting a burgeoning empire that had molded itself from scars, sacrifices, and hard-earned victories.

As I walked through the halls, I felt an overwhelming sense of pride swell within me. The Moretti family was no longer just a name steeped in shadows; we had transformed into a powerful force with roots tapping deeply into the very communities we sought to protect. Every decision, every alliance, and every moment of vulnerability had reshaped our legacy, forging a path toward a new tomorrow.

Alessia joined me, her presence radiating warmth and determination. She had become an incredible force of nature—a true partner in every sense. Together, we had laid the groundwork for a legacy that would extend beyond the world of crime. She had nurtured not only our child but the revitalized relationships that now bonded the families around us.

"Dante," she said, her voice pulling me from my thoughts. "We should discuss the dynamics with Marco and Elena."

The mention of their relationship sent a ripple of tension through me. Marco had long been like a brother to me, but his potential connection with Giovanni changed everything. Vincenzo would not quickly approve of the growing love between his daughter and Marco if Marco's father was proven to be Giovanni.

I knew this could put Marco's loyalty to the test, forcing him to navigate a web of familial ties, mistrust, and the weight of legacy.

"Let's meet in the study," I suggested, already envisioning how we could strategize from a position of strength. The winds of change were blowing fiercely, and we had to be poised to adapt.

As we settled into the familiar surroundings of the study, surrounded by leather-bound books and the weight of our family history, I couldn't shake the feeling that there were no easy answers. The consequences of Marco and Elena's relationship loomed above us like a tempest.

"Alessia, I—I want to support Marco, but I can't ignore the risks that he brings into our lives," I confessed, feeling the weight of my words settle heavily in the air. "The connection to Giovanni creates a complication. Ties like those could draw unnecessary friction to our family." I sighed heavily. "I know Elena's parents feel the same."

"I understand your concerns, Dante," she replied, leaning forward with an intensity that ignited a flicker of hope in my chest. "But Marco loves her. He believes she can forge her own path. We need to emphasize that loyalty isn't easily discarded, especially after everything we've been through together. We must navigate this with care or we risk losing them both."

Her perspective resonated deeply within me. "But we also must protect our child from any dangers that might lurk in the shadows. I can't shake the apprehension that he might be a gateway for Giovanni's influence."

"We can grant Marco the opportunity to make his own choices," Alessia said. "If we shield him, we may inadvertently push him away. Instead, let's meet with him. Encouragement could strengthen our bond and create trust, allowing him to carve out his own path while remaining committed to our family."

I nodded, recognizing the wisdom in her words. "You're right. But we'll need to be firm about the boundaries. We can't allow this relationship to compromise our position, especially now that our standing has become stronger than ever. We've built something significant—something that can shatter if we lose control of our allegiances."

She smiled, the determination in her eyes twinkling with fierce resolve. "And we will protect our family from the dangers out there. Our child deserves a world where they can grow up safe and unaware of the chaos surrounding us. Empowering Marco does not mean betraying our purpose."

As the conversation shifted, I felt a wave of clarity wash over me. We had created a magnificent legacy, but it was one that demanded vigilance and careful navigation. Shielding our child from the lurking dangers required us to strengthen our alliances rather than weaken them.

The thought of what dangers could lie ahead made my blood run cold. Like an unexpected storm, we had to anticipate threats before they emerged. The world of organized crime was not kind, and although we had forged new paths rooted in cooperation, complexities remained.

"Then we regroup with Marco soon," I said, my voice steady with conviction. "We'll approach him with compassion but with unwavering resolve. He needs to understand that his choices ripple across our family."

"Exactly," Alessia replied. "Let him know that our decisions affect not only our lives but the future of our child. We can uphold those ties while ensuring that our legacy isn't compromised."

Her support invigorated me, allowing me to channel our dedication to the child we held dear. Together, we navigated discussions about how to alleviate both familial tensions and threats, united in our commitment to see our legacy flourish while protecting what mattered most.

"Let's commit ourselves to building a safe environment," I urged, leaning closer to her as passion ignited within me. "Not just for us but for the future of all our families. We have the chance to reshape the narrative in the world around us."

The partnership we built throughout our journey had expanded into something beautiful—a legacy rooted in love, loyalty, and empowerment. As we continued to strategize in the study, a sense of calm embraced me, knowing we would face whatever came next together.

Later that evening, I made my way back through the bustling estate, alive with the joyous laughter of our allies gathered to celebrate our recent victories. The air vibrated with a sense of belonging, and I felt the promise of newfound connections strengthening our familial bonds. As I moved through the crowd, I spotted Luca, engrossed in discussion with a group of our allies—his fiery charisma embodying the spirit of unity that was burgeoning around us.

"Luca," I called, catching his attention. "Can you gather everyone in the main hall? I want to speak with all of you about the future."

He nodded, his enthusiasm contagious as he mobilized the others. I felt the energy in the room shift, camaraderie pulsing between us, and I mentally prepared for the next chapter of our legacy.

Once the hall filled with the heads of the families, I stepped forward, my heart racing with anticipation. Their collective presence symbolized a power that had been forged amid struggles and dedication. Every face in the crowd reflected alliances built on trust and respect, and it reminded me that we were stronger together.

"Thank you for gathering here tonight," I began, my voice steady as I addressed the room. "Our recent victories have paved the way toward a new horizon for all of us. I want to ensure that we not only reap the rewards of our hard work but also safeguard our future."

As I spoke about the plans to expand our influence and foster connections within the community, I noticed Alessia standing beside me, calm and confident, embodying everything we had fought for. "We will protect our children and families while establishing a legacy rooted in loyalty and strength. We will not let fear dictate our lives; rather, we will empower those around us."

A wave of agreement surged through the crowd, a collective understanding blossoming from shared experiences.

"But," I continued, shifting my focus. "There are challenges ahead, especially regarding loyalty and the dynamics of our families. In three months, Alessia and I will be married. And when that union takes place, the power of our families unite, benefiting everyone here. Now is the time to be vigilant. Report anything you see or hear that could threaten what we've built."

Whispers rippled through the room as family heads exchanged glances, acknowledging the complexities that lay ahead. I held my ground, sensing the weight of the moment.

"Together, we will ensure that every single person working for us, close or far, understands the importance of our legacy," I finished. "We will be united, ready to face whatever challenges come our way as we protect our future generation."

The energy in the room pulsed with resolve and solidarity. In that moment, I understood more profoundly that we were embarking on a new journey together, one filled with hope and determination. As I looked around at the faces of allies and friends, I gained a renewed sense of strength.

Alessia's hand rested against my back, offering silent support, and I turned to meet her gaze. I could see the same fire within her, the unyielding commitment to transforming our legacies woven together.

As the discussions intensified around the room, I felt a burden lift from my shoulders. The challenges ahead would not be easy, but I was prepared to face them. I had discovered more than just the values of loyalty and family—they were my guiding light as we moved forward, ever vigilant against the dangers that lurked in the shadows.

We were entering a new era, and I was ready to embrace it. No matter the storms we might face, we would continue to forge our path together, united against the challenges ahead. With every choice we made, we ushered in a legacy of power, strength, and unwavering love—one that would echo through the ages, igniting hope in the hearts of generations to come.

Epilogue: Grand Adventures - Alessia's POV

The world tilted the moment the chapel doors opened.

Every head turned. Every eye landed on me. But I saw only one.

Dante.

Standing at the altar in a black tailored suit and a midnight silk tie, my husband-to-be didn't just look powerful—he looked like a man who would level kingdoms for me. Claim nations. Burn through bloodlines if it meant I would be his, without hesitation or limit.

My heels clicked softly on the marble floor as I walked toward him. The veil floated behind me like smoke. The dress hugged my figure, satin and strength, ivory with Romano lace stitched at the hem. Family. Legacy. Fire.

But none of that mattered when Dante looked at me like I was not a pawn in an empire—but the prize.

I reached him. Dante's hand wrapped around mine, steady and sure.

"*Ciao, regina mia,*" he whispered.

My queen.

I stared up at him, chin high, smile restrained. But my heart was in chaos beneath the silk. Chaos and certainty.

We recited our vows. Ancient, traditional, sealed in both Latin and blood. He slid a ring on my finger—a diamond, coiled in gold filigree, inscribed inside with a phrase only I will ever read: *In chaos, I choose you.*

He lifted my veil. Kissed me slowly. Devoured my breath like it belonged to him.

Because it did.

Dante Moretti was mine. And I was his.

The crowd erupted in polite applause, but it was the smile in his eyes I felt most.

We walked out of the church under a rain of white petals and champagne toasts. The estate waited behind us, ready for the reception, but before I could even ask where we're going next, Dante curled his hand around mine and leaned into my ear.

"Come, *sposa*. Our jet is waiting."

I blinked. "Jet?"

He led me to a black car idling behind the limousines. No fanfare. No fanbase. Just us.

"You didn't think I would let you get bored in New York, did you?"

"I assumed we'd be running the East Coast together," I said as he helped me into the back seat, my dress pooling like luxury and secrets.

Dante shut the door, slid in beside me, and smiled like a man who's been planning this for far longer than I knew.

"My legacy is bigger than NYC," he said. "A vineyard. A villa. And a seat at the Italian table. It's time someone cleaned up the mess over there."

I stared at him. "You're moving me to Italy?"

He smirked. "*We* are moving to Italy. You're my wife now. My queen. And Italy needs a queen who doesn't flinch."

"What about New York?"

He lifted my hand to his lips, kissed the ring I wore. "Axel will handle New York. He's ready."

I paused. "Your half-brother who races motorcycles and charms FBI informants with dimples?"

Dante's eyes glinted with amusement. "He's not as reckless as he seems. And besides—our story isn't meant to unfold in the city."

I studied him, heartbeat ticking faster. I'd thought I was marrying into concrete and glass. Power plays and gala games. But this—this is something else.

"You should've told me," I said, soft but sharp.

"I wanted to see if you'd walk the aisle without knowing where it led."

He brushed a knuckle down my cheek. "And you did."

"Because I trusted you," I whispered.

His gaze held mine. "Then trust me now."

Silence stretched, but it was not uncomfortable.

I exhaled slowly. The idea of Italy terrified and thrilled me. A kingdom not yet conquered. A country with old blood and old enemies.

But I was not afraid of new terrain.

Not with Dante beside me.

"I'll need to learn Italian faster," I murmured.

Dante grinned, slow and sinful. "I'll tutor you. Personally."

I arched my brow. "That supposed to be foreplay?"

His hand curled around my knee. "With you, *regina*, everything is."

The car turned toward the private airport. As the city faded behind us, I realized I was not leaving a throne—I was stepping into a larger one. With a man who saw me as more than a name. More than a pawn. He saw me as his. For always.